"How can I love Felix when I feel this way about you?"

Once again his lips met hers as he murmured, "I believe we have both wanted this since our first meeting."

The kisses were at once both gentle and passionate, and Sophia hoped they would never end. At last she recognized this is what she wanted since the time he had come to her rescue. Only pride and fear had prevented her from acknowledging the fact.

They remained locked in one another's arms until a footstep nearby caused them to break apart rather abruptly. Sophia looked up in alarm to see Felix approaching them with a face like thunder. There was no doubt he had observed them in the kind of passionate embrace she had never enjoyed in his arms.

Also by Rachelle Edwards
Published by Fawcett Books:

MARYLEBONE PARK

Rachelle Edwards

FAWCETT CREST • NEW YORK

A Fawcett Crest Book
Published by Ballantine Books
Copyright © 1990 by Rachelle Edwards

Library of Congress Catalog Card Number: 90-92921

ISBN 0-449-21702-7

Manufactured in the United States of America

First Edition: June 1990

AUTHOR'S NOTE

In the time of Henry VIII Marylebone Park was a hunting park. Later it was leased as farmland, but reverted to the Crown in 1811 when it became part of the Prince Regent's grand plan for a major development of central London as far as the Houses of Parliament. The great architect Nash planned alterations to Marylebone Park, some of which were completed by 1825, and it has been known since then as Regent's Park.

One

The street was an unfamiliar one. It was darker and narrower than the fashionable shopping and residential streets of western London. This street had no elegant houses or interesting shops to recommend it. It appeared to be lined with taverns and the type of houses where the fashionable world is seldom seen.

Sophia Kingsland looked out of the carriage window with an air of anxiety before commenting to her maid, "I wonder where Baines is taking us, Lily. I told him to drive home to Manchester Square directly. I don't recognize this place at all, and I'm sure I know the route we normally take from the Strand."

"It's the traffic, ma'am," the abigail replied. "There's always so many carriages in the Strand at this time of the day. You mark my words,

Baines'll be trying to avoid the congestion and get us home the sooner."

"I'd as lief he stayed on the main thoroughfare," Sophia replied, continuing to look troubled, "even if it does take us a few more minutes to get home."

There were a great many lawless elements abroad in London of late and Sophia could not help but be aware of them. Her own father, Sir Magnus Kingsland, had spoken out on the matter the very last time he had been in the House of Lords.

He had been prompted by the incident of Lady Welton's carriage being set upon by a drunken mob in a street just off Piccadilly, and only two days earlier Sir Arthur Tompkins had had his purse stolen in broad daylight while walking in Aldgate. There was a good deal of talk about such worrying incidents, which made Sophia all the more concerned about their route.

"I trust Baines actually does know where he is taking us," she added a moment later.

"Don't fret your head, ma'am," Lily assured her, smiling smugly. "Baines is the best coachman in the whole of London. He would not see us wrong."

Sophia smiled at last. "I do not suppose you would be prejudiced about Baines, Lily," she answered, knowing that something of a romance was ensuing between the two servants.

The girl's answering blush made Sophia smile even more. "If you become leg-shackled to Mr Harcourt, ma'am . . ."

"Not if, Lily, *when*, for it is all arranged. We are actually betrothed. The announcement has been made and, mayhap, when I marry Mr. Harcourt, you will not tarry far behind us."

The maid's cheeks became even pinker. "That is what I meant to say, ma'am. It would cause the devil of a problem for us both if you are to go and live at Mr. Harcourt's house."

"Oh, I most certainly will go to live at my husband's house! It is a very fine house in Grosvenor Square, and you already know what Foxworth is like having stayed there briefly this summer."

"Baines'll still be coachman to Sir Magnus . . ."

"Ah, so that is what troubles you! I am persuaded a reasonable accord can be reached. Papa will not wish for anything to keep you two apart and I have no desire to lose an excellent maidservant."

Lily's eyes grew wide with speculation, but before she could enlarge upon the subject, a noise attracted the attention of both servant and mistress.

"What on earth can that be?" Sophia gasped, stiffening with alarm as the carriage jerked abruptly.

Both young ladies put their heads out of opposite windows to see that they were approaching a particularly disreputable-looking inn. Several ruffians were carousing outside, while others staggered drunkenly out of the door and into the road with no regard to the possibility of traffic coming by. Baines reined in the carriage horses in order not to run any of them down, although they appeared so drunk as not to notice such a possibility.

When one of the topers shouted something at Sophia, she quickly withdrew her head, saying in disgust, "Foxed at this time of the day. Who would credit such a thing?"

" 'Tis nothing out of the way, ma'am. Liquor is cheap enough and these rapscallions have little else to do with their time. My own father was a five-bottle-a-day man until he fell into the Fleet one night and drowned. I don't suppose he even knew what happened to him."

"From all I observe, Lily, we are particularly fortunate that Papa is unusually abstemious in his habits. Being a gentleman is no guarantee against rakish habits."

The drunkards were laughing and staggering over the road, and Baines had no choice but to halt the carriage, whereupon the drunken mob began to pelt it with their empty bottles.

"Lor' we're done for!" Lily cried while the equally terrified Sophia strove to maintain her own calm and patted her maid's trembling hand in a comforting gesture.

"Where is the Watch?" she asked, wide-eyed with fear as bottles and stones began to rain down on the coach.

"Useless old men!" the maid declared. "Just like the Charleys. Useless all of them!"

When a face leered at the window, Sophia gave a squeal of alarm and the maidservant became totally hysterical, distracting her mistress from the threatening situation when she was obliged to administer her own vinaigrette to her abigail.

Suddenly, as the carriage began to rock alarmingly from side to side, a pistol shot rang out, causing both ladies to be alarmed anew. However, it came as some relief when the rocking ceased and the shouting stopped. Sophia withdrew the vinaigrette as Lily's vapors calmed.

"They've gone!" Sophia gasped. "I'm fully persuaded we are saved, Lily!"

Before she could question their miraculous deliverance or even peer out of the window, the door to the carriage opened, causing both ladies to start. However, the gentleman who stood outside was quite evidently no drunken ruffian, even if his appearance did not exactly proclaim him a gentleman. Dressed in a shabby driving coat with several capes, he looked neither a gentleman nor a rapscallion. True, he appeared somewhat unshaved with a mane of black hair, which was a good deal longer and wilder than that sported by a gentleman of the *ton* nowadays, and his clothes were several years out of fashion, too.

Despite the fact it was he who had frightened away their attackers, Sophia still felt apprehensive. All manner of malcontents stalked the streets of London, and from the look of him he could easily be one of them. Lily was evidently no more assured than her mistress, for she squealed again.

"Are you two ladies harmed in any way?" their rescuer asked, and all at once Sophia was less afraid, for whatever his appearance his speech was that of a gentleman.

"No, no, indeed," she replied after a moment's startled silence.

Their rescuer climbed into the carriage then and seated himself opposite to the two passengers, seeming to fill the carriage with his presence, and neither of the two ladies could tell if it was one of good or evil. Lily seemed to have no doubt, for she pressed herself into the corner as far away from him as was possible.

Sophia was not quite so afraid. Despite the air of wildness about him, instinct told her that this man

5

was no threat, but when he gazed at her, his eyes were so dark and penetrating she felt something of a shock; although she could not for anything understand why his look disturbed her so. However, his dark eyes, which surveyed her without expression, were very disturbing and she felt instinctively he could be dangerous if he so chose.

His scrutiny of her was so thorough, all at once Sophia saw herself as he must, dressed in the very latest style in a blue pelisse braided and with epaulets in the current military fashion. Her bonnet was a feminine version of the soldier's shako, and a certain number of fair curls were peeking out from beneath the brim.

She knew that her blue eyes must still be wide with fear and uncertainty, and she summoned up all her courage in order to sit up straight and meet his eyes boldly, which was suddenly not so easy.

"Are you quite certain you are unharmed, ma'am?" he asked, glancing at the abigail as he spoke.

Even though his manner revealed nothing sympathetic, his words did and Sophia was able to relax a little more. "Oh, yes indeed, sir. None of the ruffians entered the carriage, although I'm persuaded they would have done so if you had not interceded on our behalf so promptly."

"That, at least, is a blessing, ma'am."

"And, naturally, I am most obliged to you."

His eyes narrowed somewhat then. "Your menfolk must be criminally negligent to allow you abroad with no more protection than an unarmed driver."

Sophia looked outraged. "We did not intend to

cross Hounslow Heath, only to visit Mr. Chalmer's circulating library in the Strand." Her gloved hand tightened upon the book that had been lying at her side. "Mama had ordered a copy of *Pride and Prejudice* and she was determined to read it before Lady Abbotsbury obtained *her* copy. Much to Mama's chagrin, she always reveals the story."

Suddenly Sophia bit her lip, realizing that the shock to her nerves had evidently caused her to chatter too much. As her voice died away, she thought she detected a hint of amusement in the stranger's eyes, but a moment later it had gone, if, indeed, it had ever been there.

"Now I am assured beyond doubt that you are unharmed I believe you may go safely on your way. I intend to instruct your driver his directions."

He began to get out of the carriage and when he moved, Lily recoiled. Sophia could not know if their rescuer had noticed the gesture, but feeling guilty herself for doubting him, she blurted out:

"I shall be forever in your debt, sir."

He paused to consider her for a long, uncomfortable moment and then, in a gesture that was totally unexpected, he bent to kiss her full on the lips.

Lily gasped. Sophia was so shocked by the unexpectedness of the assault she said and did absolutely nothing.

"Consider the debt discharged, ma'am," he told her as he climbed down and closed the carriage door behind him.

The abigail suddenly recovered her wits and pushed the vinaigrette toward her mistress just as the carriage set off once again. Sophia pushed it

7

away, stunned by what had happened, but not in the least inclined to indulge in an attack of the vapors. In fact, she wondered if the entire incident had been a particularly vivid dream. Only the feel of his lips, which still lingered on hers, made her believe it had actually happened.

In order to reassure herself, she glanced out of the rear window, but she could see no sign of the man, just a number of drunks insensible at the side of the street. She had never been kissed like that before. Felix, whom she would marry at the end of the current Season, had only kissed her after their betrothal, and never in such a manner to make her lips tingle as they did now.

"Oh, Miss Kingsland, what a thing to happen," Lily lamented. "What will Sir Magnus and Lady Kingsland say when they come to hear of it?"

Sophia then snapped out of her abstraction to look sharply at her maidservant. "You will not tell them of it, Lily. You will not tell anyone, not Baines or any of the servants. Is that clearly understood?"

The maidservant looked startled, for the sharp tone in her mistress's voice was most unusual. Miss Kingsland had such an amiable nature.

"Yes, ma'am, but Baines . . . He is bound to report the incident to Sir Magnus."

"The incident, yes, but he knows nothing more. Whatever else occurred here inside the carriage must not be mentioned on any account. No one will ever know of it."

"Well, you may rely upon my discretion, ma'am."

Despite the reassurance, Sophia felt bound to underscore the matter even further. "No one can possibly hear of it if you stay mumchance, and I shall know who I must blame if I come to hear of it from any of the other servants, for only you and I were present."

"There is the gentleman, ma'am. He knows about it."

Sophia dabbed at her hot brow with a handkerchief soaked in eau de cologne. "His actions surely prove that he is no gentleman, Lily, and I am relieved to say we are not like to encounter him again."

When she glanced out of the window, she noted, with great relief, they were now traveling along Oxford Street. "I shall never again complain of the amount of carriages clogging up the roads whenever we venture out in the future," she declared.

Then she transferred her attention to her maidservant again. "I do hope I have made myself clear on the subject of what occurred here a while ago, Lily. It was an outrage against my person and there is no knowing what Papa will do if he comes to hear of it, so on that account alone I simply do not wish to be reminded of it ever again."

Two

Forgetting the incident was not as easy as Sophia had supposed. Not having it mentioned was no guarantee of not being reminded of being kissed in so round a manner by the dark stranger. Everytime she closed her eyes, it was to recall the stranger's lips so insistent upon hers. Moreover, she began to feel guilty whenever she was in Felix Harcourt's company for even thinking of the oafish stranger.

Dear, dear Felix, she thought. He was a true gentleman. He, too, would have gone with no hesitation to the rescue of any female in distress, but he would never, ever, behave in anything but the most gentlemanly manner.

When Sophia found herself seeking nonexistent signs of the servants knowing what had happened, she realized her nerves had been overset by the episode far more than she had been willing to acknowledge, and she resolved once and for all to put it out of her mind, concentrating instead on the wonderful future she was to enjoy as Mrs. Felix Harcourt.

On the day following the incident, while her younger sister, Jessica, played a desultory tune on the spinet, Sophia pored over the fashion plates in the latest edition of *La Belle Assemblée*, marking those she wished her mantua-maker to copy. Since her come out, she had attended no end of social functions and it was necessary to have a good many gowns.

"I am so relieved you are to marry Felix Harcourt," Jessica ventured at last and her sister looked up from her deliberations, smiling as she did so.

"I am so glad you like him dearest."

"He is so amiable one cannot help but like him, but there is another reason I am so happy for you."

"Oh . . . ?"

"I am delighted that you have received an offer congenial to you so soon after your come out. It must be so humiliating not to have anyone come up to scratch during one's first Season."

"I daresay you are correct, but in all truth I had not considered the possibility of that happening to me."

"That is because you had no cause to concern yourself. As I recall, Felix Harcourt was entranced by you from the very beginning, but only think how awful it must be for poor Rosie Amton and Kate Linfield. I am persuaded they are both firmly on the shelf."

Sophia smiled dreamily. "I am bound to own I

have been most fortunate in winning his affection so soon after my come out."

Jessica Kingsland paused in her playing. "It is fortunate for the both of us, you must own, for when you are married at the end of the Season, it will leave the field clear for me to make a brilliant match *next* Season. Moreover, it can do my chances no harm whatsoever if my sister is the future Viscountess Rexton."

Sophia laughed for the very first time since her awful experience. "You will need no help, my dear. You attract a deal of attention now before you are even out, just as I did."

The door to the drawing room opened and Lady Kingsland came bustling in. "My dear," she addressed her elder daughter, "we are still in a fidge over what happened to you yesterday. Your papa has instructed Baines on his future conduct of the carriage whenever any of us are abroad. It is most alarming when one cannot go about one's business without the fear of assault."

Sophia groaned silently. There was little chance of her being able to forget what happened when it had already become a great topic of conversation among her mother's acquaintances. The tattle-baskets had talked of little else since it happened, and her mother had fussed endlessly. It was not surprising that the news of the incident had spead round the beau monde with the speed of a fire. It was a great blessing that they did not know the whole of it, and Sophia could not help but smile to herself. She had few secrets from her family, but this most certainly would remain a closely guarded one.

Her mother looked relieved, mistaking Sophia's smile. "Oh, you are being so brave. Everyone is so admiring of you, my dear. Such fortitude!"

"I don't wish to be admired, Mama. I only wish for it to be forgotten as swiftly as possible."

"We cannot forget it so easily, Sophia. Moreover, it would be foolish for us to do so. It is necessary to learn a lesson from what occurred and ensure we are all safe in future whenever we venture outdoors. The matter could have been far more serious. I don't believe you are fully aware of that, my dear. I shudder to think . . . if that stranger had not . . ."

Jessica left the spinet and bounded across the room toward them, her eyes wide with speculation. "Oh, how I wish I had been there, Sophia! How romantic it must have been to have been rescued by a dark stranger!"

Sophia laughed disparagingly. "It was no such thing, I assure you. It was exceedingly alarming."

"Jessica, don't be such a goosecap," Lady Kingsland scolded and the girl looked abashed. "This is a matter of the utmost seriousness. Papa is insisting that Baines is armed with a pistol in future and does not on any account stray from the main roads."

"He was only avoiding being held up by the huge amount of carriages in the Strand," Sophia excused.

"Nevertheless, you may be sure Papa has given Baines a severe trimming. He is determined that no chances will be taken whenever any of us venture abroad. Papa only regrets you did not ask the name of the gentleman who came to your aid. He would dearly like to thank him."

"So would I," Jessica said, glancing mischievously at her sister, who was unable to prevent a flood of color creeping up her cheeks.

"I did thank him," Sophia assured her.

"Well, from all you have told us, it is evident he would have welcomed a small reward for his pains. It would have been the very least we could have done to express our extreme gratitude. However, it is useless to express regrets. What is done is done."

"Indeed," Sophia sighed.

"We must just ensure that it never occurs again."

"Indeed," Sophia concurred, keeping her eyes averted.

"If ever you encounter the fellow in the future, you must ask him to call upon Papa," Lady Kingsland insisted to her daughter's alarm.

"It is most unlike I would encounter him again, Mama, especially as Baines is now forbidden to stray from the main thoroughfare."

"I daresay that is so," Lady Kingsland admitted, much to Sophia's relief.

"That gown is so like your new Indian cotton," Jessica remarked, indicating the fashion plate that Sophia had been contemplating in the magazine when their mother had arrived.

"So it is," Sophia replied, glad of an opportunity to change the subject at last.

Lady Kingsland stood up. "Recall that Mr. Harcourt is calling to take you riding in the Park at five," she reminded her elder daughter.

"As if I am like to forget," Sophia answered wryly.

As usual when her future husband was mentioned, a faint tinge of pink rose in her cheeks.

"It is evident Sophia is in a fidge to be with him,

Mama," Jessica confided, "for she has been Friday-faced all afternoon."

"That is nothing out of the ordinary," her mother informed her as Sophia cast her sister a disgusted look.

"That is totally unfair!" Sophia protested.

"No one will think it amiss if you act the mooncalf," Jessica reminded her. "You are, after all, only recently betrothed to the most amiable man alive."

"Do not gammon your sister," Lady Kingsland admonished. "If her sensibilities are overset, it is no wonder. She has been obliged to endure a good deal of late. Betrothed and held up by ruffians all in a sennight. 'Tis a wonder we did not have to burn feathers!"

Jessica looked mutinous as her mother swept out of the room. "I am truly beginning to feel the slightest ennui on the subject of your little adventure."

"Then you would oblige us all by not mentioning it again," Sophia snapped.

"That is all very well, but there are countless others who will insist upon mentioning it, at least until the next sensation occurs." Sophia drew a profound sigh, knowing this to be true. Jessica was gazing at her sister, who affected to read the magazine. "You have become decidedly toplofty since you became engaged to marry Felix Harcourt."

"And you, my dear, have become a chucklehead," Sophia responded, smiling with false sweetness.

The embryonic quarrel was stopped by the arrival of Celia Waddell, one of Sophia's bosom friends.

"My dear," she cried, her bonnet feathers

aquiver, "I have only just heard of your terrible ordeal!"

Sophia sighed once again acknowledging that her sister was, of course, correct. She was not going to be allowed to forget, at least not until another sensational occurrence superseded it in the gossip-starved echelons of the beau monde.

"Celia, one would not believe a ferocious war was being fought on the Continent. By comparison, I assure you what happened to me was of very little account."

Miss Waddell looked at Jessica and then back to her friend. "Oh, how brave of you to say so, but you must tell me all. I intend to hear the tale from your own lips so I know the truth of the matter and not what Emily Bagly chooses to tell me."

With as much brevity as she could muster, Sophia recounted the adventure while her sister continued to sulk. Sophia could well understand her ire; she knew full well in normal circumstances she could tolerate Jessica's teasing with good humor.

"Incroyable!" Miss Waddell exclaimed. "How utterly terrifying for you, my dear, but what of the mysterious gentleman who interceded so heroically on your behalf? You have not even mentioned him."

Sophia smiled. "There is nothing to tell."

"How so?"

"It was over so quickly there was no opportunity to make his acquaintance before he was on his way once more."

"*I* should have insisted upon knowing his name at the very least."

"So should I," Jessica interpolated.

16

"I own I was anxious only to be away from the scene," Sophia explained, not for the first time.

"That is understandable, but do tell me . . ." Miss Waddell looked suddenly coy. "Was he very handsome?"

A fleeting vision of his handsome features passed through Sophia's mind, but then she almost shuddered to think of the story being repeated in the salons of the *ton*. A moment later she affected an air of nonchalance.

"I'm sure I did not notice."

"I cannot credit that!" Miss Waddell gasped.

"In similar circumstances I doubt if you would have done differently," Sophia pointed out.

"I don't doubt my sister's mind was full of Mr. Harcourt at the time," Jessica broke in, not troubling to hide her sarcasm.

"No doubt," Miss Waddell agreed. "You may be interested to know I caught sight of Mr. Harcourt driving his high-perch phaeton in Bond Street a short while ago."

"It's possible he was visiting his tailor," Sophia answered absently, relieved to be talking of Felix and not the dark stranger.

"Or Gentleman Jackson's Gymnasium," Jessica broke in.

Sophia smiled genuinely now. "Indeed. He is fond of training in the art of fisticuffs."

"He should be arriving here very soon if he is to take you riding in Hyde Park," Jessica pointed out.

Sophia began to relax a little more, for a ride with Felix in Hyde Park at the fashionable hour was bound to soothe her bruised sensibilities more than anything else was likely to do.

"Bringing Mr. Harcourt up to scratch has made you the envy of all the other debutantes," her friend confided. "I am sure it will be no time at all before he becomes Viscount Rexton. His papa ails, you know."

"Being married to Felix will suffice, Celia, I assure you. I am looking forward to making my home at Foxworth. It is the most beautiful house I have ever seen."

"Mr. Harcourt offered for Sophia as soon as she came out," Jessica informed Miss Waddell and there was no mistaking the pride in her voice.

The other young lady dimpled. "It must have been decided earlier than the start of the Season, I fancy."

"It's no secret we were invited to Foxworth during the summer, and Felix and I were in each other's company a great deal during the stay."

"There was never any doubt *you* would make a favorable match, even though I am bound to declare blond hair is a trifle out of fashion this Season," Miss Waddell told her.

Sophia was not in the least put out by the declaration as she replied, "Now, you must tell me, Celia, are you any nearer to bringing Captain Murchison up to scratch, if it is he you still favor?"

Miss Waddell giggled. "Oh, indeed, I have not changed my mind on that score. I am persuaded you may expect an announcement very soon."

Sophia had no opportunity to congratulate her friend before a footman arrived bearing a note for her.

"A billet-doux from Sir Thomas Cawthorne, perchance?" Miss Waddell suggested slyly, referring to one of Sophia's other suitors.

Sophia smiled sweetly as she broke the wafer. "Sir Thomas is now well aware that my affections are engaged elsewhere. Oh dear . . ." she gasped as she scanned the note.

"Not bad news, I trust," Miss Waddell inquired, her expression eager as she looked at her friend.

"On the contrary, it is not bad news at all, except that Mr. Harcourt cannot, after all, ride with me in the Park today, and I was looking forward to it greatly."

"Crying off so soon after the announcement," Miss Waddell declared. "Pray, what is good news about that?"

"You may be certain the reason he has cried off is fully justified," Sophia explained. "It appears his cousin has returned to London, and Felix is in a fidge to see him with no delay."

Miss Waddell's brow furrowed, which her friend understood, for there was little that happened in London circles that she did not know.

"His cousin? I don't . . ."

"His name is Lord Manville, if that means anything to you, Celia. He went to the Peninsula with Wellington's expeditionary force and tragically was grievously wounded at Cuidad Rodrigo."

The young lady's brow cleared at last. "Ah yes. Lord Manville. I have yet to make his acquaintance, but I have heard talk of him."

"So have I, but in truth not a great deal," Sophia admitted. "Felix speaks of him in so fond a manner I feel I do know him. He has always been something

19

of a hero to Felix, being somewhat older. Now I daresay he will be a hero to all."

Miss Waddell nodded sagely. "I have heard Mama make mention of Lord Manville. Indeed, I believe I heard her say only yesterday that London will be livelier now that he is returned to town. I confess I did not heed her words at the time. Tell me what you know of him. I had no notion he was Felix Harcourt's cousin."

"I know little more than you," Sophia admitted. "He was grievously injured in the battle. Indeed, they despaired of his life, and his recovery is regarded as something of a miracle."

"According to the *on-dits*, I have heard he is hideously deformed."

"I should not at all be surprised," Sophia affirmed. "His horse fell upon him during a cavalry charge and broke many of the bones in his body."

Jessica, who had been listening avidly, gasped, "How did he survive such a thing?"

"Felix says he has the devil's own luck in everything."

"Well, it is very evident he cannot be as he was," Miss Waddell ventured. "Why else would Merinda Whitchurch marry another when she was betrothed to Lord Manville, who was known to be quite a catch. Mama tells me that despite his reputation as a rake, scores of females dangled after him for several Seasons, and there was copious weeping when Merinda Whitchurch accepted his offer."

Sophia looked astounded. "Lady Whitchurch! Betrothed to Felix's cousin! This is a great surprise to me, Celia. I truly had no notion."

20

Miss Waddell looked well pleased. It was always so very satisfying to be the first with news, especially as so many gossips tended to spoil such coups.

"You must persuade Mr. Harcourt to tell you all about his cousin, Sophia. It is evident to me he has been exceedingly remiss. I should have wanted to know *everything* if I were in your place. Lord Manville is known as the scapegrace of the family and, as such, of the utmost interest."

She gathered together her gloves and reticule and made to go. "I have dallied far longer than I intended. Lord Hendricks is taking me riding in the Park and I fear he will already be cooling his heels."

Sophia looked puzzled. "Did you not say that Captain Murchison . . . ?"

Miss Waddell grinned wickedly. "Indeed I did, but as the announcement is not yet made, I may as well make the most of my come-out year before I become a boringly sober matron."

"That will never be true of you, Celia," her friend responded.

"I daresay it will be true of all of us before too long."

Sophia was still smiling when her mother returned some few minutes later. "Did I not see Celia Waddell leaving just now?"

"You did indeed, Mama."

"I scarce need to guess what she wanted—all the gory details of your little adventure, no doubt."

"There were no gory details, Mama!"

"That child is such a tattle-basket. Sophia, should you not be preparing for Felix's arrival? He will be here at any time now." Sophia showed her mother the note. "Gone to see Lord Manville? How odd. I thought he was dead, or mayhap that was Lord Greville."

"Apparently he is very much alive, miraculously so," Sophia answered. "Did you know him before he went to the Peninsula, Mama?"

"Oh, indeed I did. Who did not? It was impossible to ignore that young man however hard one tried. He was worthy of being called a rakehell if ever anyone was. His cronies called him Hellfire Manville, if you please!"

"I had no notion," Sophia replied laughingly.

"You were still in the schoolroom at the time, I am glad to say. No young lady was exempt from his charm, and a good many older ones, too! His poor papa did not know what to do with him because of his drinking, gaming, and fighting, not to mention . . . well everything to excess. Sadly, I daresay, his rakehell days are over now. He was hideously injured, you know."

"He does not seem to me to be the type of gentleman who would take his injuries well," Sophia said thoughtfully as she nibbled on a piece of marchpane.

"He sounds a most interesting gentleman to me," Jessica remarked. "I would dearly like to make his acquaintance."

Lady Kingsland smiled mirthlessly. "Before he was commissioned into his regiment, I would not have wanted him in the vicinity of either of my daughters, I assure you."

Sophia smiled and Jessica laughed out loud. "That makes him all the more interesting to me, Mama," the younger girl pointed out.

Her mother smiled sagely. "There were a good many foolish females who regretted such feelings, I assure you, my dear."

The girl's eyes sparkled with mischief. "Are you certain you wish Sophia to marry a member of his family if they are as rackety as you say?"

Lady Kingsland looked askance at her younger daughter. "Felix Harcourt is a splendid young man, kin or not. The entire family is exceedingly worthy apart from Lord Manville, who has appeared to have redeemed himself somewhat in the Peninsula."

"I agree that Felix could not be more splendid," Sophia said, looking all at once dreamy.

Lady Kingsland sighed profoundly. "I daresay Merinda Daley knew what she was about when she married Freddie Whitchurch instead of Lord Manville. If there was any hope at all for his lordship to live a normal life, she would not, in my opinion, have married another. I don't suppose I need concern myself about my daughters now, for I am persuaded Lord Manville is no longer a threat to any young lady."

She started toward the door. "I cannot spend any more time chattering. I must go and speak to Cook and check that everything is in order for tomorrow's rout."

As she breezed out of the room, Jessica looked at her sister with interest. "Do *you* think Lord Manville has returned a cripple?"

"I don't know. I don't believe that Felix knows either and that is why he is so anxious to call upon him."

"No doubt you will be engaged to call upon the invalid before long."

Sophia looked at once alarmed. "Oh, do you think so?"

"Don't you?"

Sophia sighed. "I daresay you are correct, dearest. If I don't meet him myself in the course of the next few days, I suppose someone else will make it their business to call upon him, and then the *on-dit* will be all over town. Lord Manville's miserable situation will be known in the smallest detail to one and all."

Jessica looked thoughtful. "It does seem so sad to think of him being so much of an invalid after enjoying an active life in every field. He must still be relatively young, too."

Once again Sophia drew a sigh. "There are so many crippled soldiers, Jessica, and like to be more if this infernal war isn't over soon."

"It cannot possibly last much longer. After the victory at Vittoria, Boney is on the run at last. Everyone says peace has never been closer."

"I do trust you are correct, dearest," Sophia replied before picking up her sewing.

As she concentrated on the intricate stitches, she became hopeful that because Felix's interesting cousin was back in town, everyone would now forget what had happened to her.

Three

As Mr. Felix Harcourt drove along Park Lane, he was unable to give full rein to the splendid team that pulled his phaeton, owing to the many other carriages making their way to Hyde Park for the daily promenade. He could not help but experience a feeling of deep regret that he could not go riding with Sophia on that particular afternoon, but as he had not set eyes on his cousin for several years, he felt duty-bound to call upon him with no possible delay.

He was a fine-looking young man, although of only average height with closely cropped hair and bright hazel eyes. He had learned well his clothes sense from his cousin, who patronized only the very best tailor and boot maker. It was generally acknowledged that he and Miss Sophia Kingsland were a well-matched pair.

His destination, Manville House, was one of the

finest mansions on Park Lane with a courtyard at the front into which Mr. Harcourt drove his carriage and pair. The moment the groom took charge of the team, the young man jumped down and strode into the house where he was immediately divested of his hat, caped driving coat, and gloves.

"It is good to see you again," he told the house steward, who greeted him warmly.

"And you Master . . . Mr. Harcourt. It is just like it was used to be before his lordship went abroad."

Privately the young man doubted life could ever be that carefree again for his cousin, but he forbore to say so.

Instead he asked, "How is Lord Manville today, Potter?"

"I am glad to say his lordship is in excellent spirits, sir."

"Whenever is he not?" Felix replied, looking suddenly anxious.

"His lordship is in the library, sir, and has instructed me to take you to him immediately when you arrive."

As Felix Harcourt followed the house steward up the stairs, he was very much apprehensive about what he would find once he was reunited with the earl. He had only been a boy when he had last seen Patrick Manville, whose wild ways had appeared heroic to such a callow youth. After the horrific events at Cuidad Rodrigo, Felix Harcourt dreaded to see a change in his cousin. If he had returned to anything less than full health, it would be a terrible burden for his cousin to bear.

The library at Manville House was familiar to him. Before Patrick went away, Felix had often called in from his own house in Grosvenor Square in the hope of seeing his cousin. More often than not Lord Manville, then Viscount Langdale, had been on his way to or returning from a mill, or horse race. Frequently he had been suffering a hangover or a set-down from his father, the late earl. Felix never tired of hearing his cousin talk about his exploits, which both enraged and excited his peers. It was one scandal after another that horrified the beau monde, but which certainly amused Felix.

The young man walked into the library rather hesitantly, fearful of what he would see. For a moment or two he could see no one in the rather dark interior, but then a movement at the far side of the room caught his attention.

"Felix!" a familiar voice called out, as strong and as vigorous as ever it had been.

When his cousin came to greet him, Felix was amazed to see him actually walking toward him. He was still taller than Felix, although there were now a few silver strands in those dark tresses that many females thought so romantic. As he came down the room toward him, Felix's worried expression was transformed into a beaming smile.

"Patrick! How wonderful to see you! You've scarcely changed at all!"

The two men embraced briefly before the earl held Felix away from him. "You have, by jove! My little coz has grown up into a real bang-up blade! Who would have thought it?"

"Fie to me, Patrick. Let's look at you. Why, you've scarce changed. It's true! You're a little older, perhaps, which is not surprising after all you have been obliged to endure."

27

The older man's smile faded a little. "That is all in the past, I am glad to say. It was hellish for a while, I confess, but there are great hopes it will soon be at an end. Wellington is a great man. He will beat Boney if anyone can. Come, Felix, I have a bottle of Madeira wine here and we shall make up for lost times."

"That's splendid. I have been so concerned for you, but now I could not be happier."

"How is my uncle?" the earl inquired.

"Gouty," Felix replied, "but otherwise well."

"I will call upon him as soon as I am able."

"He will be glad to see you. He was always used to find you devilishly diverting."

The earl looked momentarily pensive. "How odd that is, Felix, when I drove my own father to distraction."

"No doubt Father would not have countenanced such behavior in me!"

"You are, and always have been, a credit to your family, unlike your scapegrace coz."

Felix laughed. "By all accounts you have redeemed yourself in recent times."

The earl ushered him toward the fire where a decanter and glasses had been set upon a silver salver on a small table. Felix Harcourt seated himself while his cousin poured the wine.

"As you can see, I came as soon as I received your note," the young man told him. "In truth I had no notion you were in town. No one else can have done, else I would have heard of it."

"I have, in fact, been here for several days," Lord Manville replied as he handed Felix his glass.

They both raised their glasses and Felix said, "To

28

your triumphant return, Patrick, and a happy one. It certainly is a happy occasion for me."

They drank of the wine and Felix went on a moment later, "If you were here days ago, why on earth didn't you send to tell me earlier?"

The earl did not sit down. He stood to one side of the fireplace, one elbow on the mantel beneath the Romney painting of his late mother.

"You will be obliged to forgive me the omission. I needed a few days to set myself to rights." One hand strayed to his elegant Brutus hairstyle. "Time to visit my barber, tailor, and so on. How I looked was not as I wished to be seen by my family and acquaintances."

Felix smiled his understanding of the situation. "I cannot tell you how relieved I am to see you like this. The tattle-baskets had you for a cripple. In truth I was in a quake until I was able to reassure myself just now."

"As you see—the whole man." The earl refilled both their glasses. "It is good to be back in England if only for the wine."

"You haven't changed a bit," Felix assured him, enjoying the excellent quality of the liquor.

The early smiled grimly. "War changes everything, Felix."

"Do you want to talk about it?"

"No."

"Damn it, Patrick, by all accounts you were crippled at the very least. I came here today feeling the greatest trepidation as to your situation."

"Patrick Manville in a Bath chair—never!" The earl sighed and looked at his cousin. "During that last assault, a cannon blew up my mount and the

29

poor devil unseated me, which would not have been so serious except I ended up beneath the carcass."

"Good grief!"

"When the battle was over, I was left until last to be treated owing to the gravity of the injuries. No one was in any doubt I had been given notice to quit. For a while I believed it, too, but I confounded them all, Felix, and here I am."

"I am amazed and full of admiration for you."

All the while he had been speaking, the earl had looked grim, but when he looked at his cousin again he was smiling. "Well, that is all in the past, for me at least. Now I look to you to keep me abreast of all that has happened in town in my absence."

"All," Felix echoed with a laugh. " 'Tis not possible, I fear."

"I know a good deal has happened since I left London. It appears our king has finally lost his reason and Prinny has his long-awaited Regency at last. Poor devil!"

"Brummell and he are not speaking now. It is as well for you to know. I would not wish you to pull a boner."

Lord Manville drained his glass and set it on the table. To his cousin's surprise, he did not fill it up again. "As it happens, I do know about their estrangement. Before I came up to town, Prinny invited me to Brighton. He takes a keen interest in the war and wished to be briefed by me personally. My Lady Hertford was also there and Princess Charlotte, who I fear is a trifle too plump to be a beauty. I was at the Marine Pavilion to see the mock battle Prinny always enjoys in August. It was most diverting."

Felix laughed. "You was never used to be diverted by such pedestrian adventures."

"Life has been tedious since I returned. I look forward to being further diverted now I'm back in town."

"That sounds like my coz," Felix laughingly replied. "But you are not as out of touch as I supposed."

"There was no shortage of females willing to write to tell me all the *on-dits*, even if they were somewhat out of date before I received their letters."

There was a note of bitterness in his voice and Felix said quickly, "Your return to social circles is bound to cause some degree of excitement among the ladies of the *ton*."

"If only to ascertain the extent of my infirmity."

"No, Patrick, not for that, and you know it. The presence of Patrick Manville is like to excite a good deal of interest. Are you going to enliven the boring social round as you used to do?"

'We shall see," the earl answered enigmatically. "So much has changed."

"Not basically, I assure you."

The earl shrugged slightly. "Since I left for the Peninsula, Drury Lane has reopened, the divine Sarah Siddons has retired, and that popinjay Byron, I am told, is quite famous for his poetry. That is the most amazing thing of all."

"Oh, yes, he causes ructions in much the same way you used to do."

"Oh, surely not!"

"He certainly has not your style, Patrick, but he does have a talent to outrage. He spoke in the Lords a while ago against making frame-braking a capital offense. I am glad to report to you his plea was not accepted and we no longer have any problem with the Luddites."

"Who would have thought it of him?"

"You would have been diverted by his affair with William Lamb's wife, Caro. It was conducted quite publicly, much to everyone's amusement. Of course, Caro Lamb is even more outrageous than he."

Felix drained his glass and then hesitated to refill it in the face of his cousin's newfound abstemiousness. "In any event it is over now and he has a new *chère amie*, none other than Lady Oxford who outraged Prinny by dining with Princess Caroline a while ago."

He considered his cousin carefully for a moment or two before adding, "Yes, I can see by your appearance you have been exceedingly busy since your return to Town."

The earl laughed for the first time and Felix glimpsed something of the devil-may-care cousin he once admired so much. Lord Manville took up one of the jeweled snuffboxes from the table and offered it to the younger man. Felix took a pinch and a moment later his cousin did so, too.

"Excellent blend, Patrick," the young man told him. "It is evident you have lost little time in patronizing your favorite establishments."

"With very good reason," the earl replied. "If only you had seen me when I first arrived. Prinny was outraged when he saw me in Brighton. If anyone else had seen me, they'd have considered me ruined by war. I was shabby enough to be mistaken for a tatterdemalion."

Felix laughed, shaking his head in disbelief. "You! Never! Even in dishabille you would be recognized for the arbiter elegantiarum you are. I am envious of your boots, Patrick. They are splendid."

"No one can make a pair as well as Hoby, but the fellow grows more impudent as time goes on. I had quite forgotten about it."

"I don't doubt your wit will confound the fellow, and one must make allowances for his genius."

There followed a brief pause after which the earl did refill both their glasses. Then he observed his cousin gravely for a moment or two before he said:

"We have spoken of what has happened to me, and in the beau monde, but what of you, Felix? We haven't spoken of you, and when I left England you were not much more than a boy. Now you are a man and by all accounts about to acquire yourself a wife."

Felix was savoring a mouthful of wine. When he swallowed it he said, "I am the most fortunate of men, Patrick. Sophia is an angel."

"It pleases me to see you so happy."

"There can be no man happier than I, and I cannot wait for you to meet her."

'I shall look forward to it, Felix, you may be sure." He considered the younger man for a moment or two before continuing, "As delighted as I am for your felicity, in truth it has come as a surprise to me to learn you intend to become legshackled at such a youthful age."

Felix Harcourt smiled smugly as he enjoyed his wine. "If you had met Sophia, you would not doubt my reasons, Patrick, and in any event I am scarce younger than you when you and . . ."

His voice died away suddenly. "I am so sorry. I did not mean to remind you of something that must still be painful to you."

The earl had been staring into the fire while his cousin spoke, but now he looked up and his face betrayed no emotion. "You need not beg my pardon on that score, Felix. The jade is of no consequence to me now."

"It is a great relief to me to hear you say so. I believe the lady is the loser."

The earl's eyes narrowed. "Oh?"

"If it is any consolation to you, she and Whitchurch often quarrel in public. I do not believe they are in the least suited."

"That was also said when she and I became betrothed."

"You would have tamed her hoydenish ways, Patrick."

"My offer for her was my father's notion, not mine. He thought a marriage would tame *me*. If you recall at the time, I was in the devil of a fix. I'd run up some horrendous debts and then there was the duel with Smythe, who lost his arm as a consequence."

"If anyone ever deserved to be called out and trounced, Smythe did."

His cousin smiled faintly. "Well, it is all past and done, and Merinda Daley did me a great service in marrying Whitchurch in my stead. She is as faithless as most females."

Felix drained the last of his wine and then got to his feet. "Not all, Patrick, not all," he assured him as he glanced at his gold hunter before returning it to his pocket. "I regret I am obliged to leave you now. I am engaged to attend a card party this evening. It will be a dreadful squeeze, but one is obliged to put in an appearance."

"Of course," his cousin agreed.

"While I have it in mind, I would like to make mention of the fact that my future in-laws are giving a rout tomorrow evening, and I know they would be delighted for you to attend."

"Mayhap—if Weston delivers my evening clothes in time."

"I insist that you come, Patrick. Apart from Papa, you are my closest relative and I am in a fidge for you to meet Sophia and to share our happiness." He fumbled in his pocket for a moment or two before bringing out an object that he handed to his cousin. "Sophia gave me this miniature when we became betrothed. It is an excellent likeness."

As the earl took the miniature from him, Felix went on, "Mr. Lawrence is at present painting a full-length portrait of her, which will hang at Foxworth in the Ladies' Gallery after we are married. I intend to engage him to paint a portrait of us as a couple and that will hang in the great hall of the house in Grosvenor Square."

As his cousin spoke the earl gazed at Sophia's likeness for some few moments. When he handed it back to Felix, there was no telling expression on his face, but he said, "There is no doubt your future bride is a great beauty. I do hope she will continue to make you happy, Felix."

As the young man pocketed the miniature once again, he laughed and slapped his cousin heartily on the back. "Oh, Patrick, you sound so doubtful, and I am bound to acknowledge I understand your reasons, based upon your most unfortunate experience with Miss Daley. Before the Season is over, I'll wager you will have won the heart of some fair maid, who will restore your faith in matters of the heart."

The earl raised his eyes to meet those of his cousin. "And I'll wager you that by the end of the Season you will have discovered Miss Kingsland to be as faithless as the rest of her gender."

Felix stiffened with anger. "Watch your words, Patrick."

Some of the old devilish light came into the earl's eyes then. "You cannot be so certain of Miss Kingsland or you would wager a thousand guineas on her fidelity."

"Damn it! You insult my bride-to-be and, if it were not for our relationship and all the dreadful hardships you have been obliged to bear, my reaction to your words would be quite different, I assure you."

"A duel you mean? I can still kill at twenty paces, I'll have you know."

"You must stop this, Patrick, now!"

Suddenly the earl threw back his head and roared with laughter. "It is evident you are no gamester, Felix. Let us forget my foolish words. I was only gammoning you. Don't you recall how it was used to be with us?"

Felix smiled faintly as his cousin escorted him downstairs, their relationship cordial once again. As the young man donned his coat and hat, he happened to glimpse out of the corner of his eye some movement on the stairs. When he looked up in the direction of the movement, he was surprised to see a figure darting back into the shadows. It could well have been a curious maidservant, but Felix somehow doubted it.

When he looked at the earl again, his cousin said, a mite shamefacedly, which was out of character, "You have caught me out, Felix."

"We never used to have secrets between us."

"I have no wish to keep this one from you."

The earl called out in a foreign tongue, which Felix recognized as Spanish, and the most exquisite-looking girl he had ever clapped eyes upon came slowly down the stairs. Lord Manville went to meet her at the bottom of the staircase, speaking to her softly in Spanish. She was wearing a gown of red satin overlaid with black lace in a style that Felix assumed to be Spanish, for it looked nothing like those he had seen worn by ladies of his acquaintance.

"Felix, allow me to present to you Senorita Malliende. Manuela Malliende."

The girl curtsied and Felix drew on his driving gloves. "It is evident I need not, after all, have any fears for your love life, Patrick."

The earl laughed softly and with a few words sent the girl upstairs again. "It is nothing of the kind, although there are few who would believe it. That is why I am keeping her a secret for the present. Senorita Malliende is a dancer, Felix, a wonderful dancer. She is going to take the *ton* by storm when she appears on the stage, I promise you, but I beg of you keep mumchance on this until I have arranged a suitable chaperon for her."

"That will make no odds. You have a formidable

reputation with the ladies so as you have rightly said, it is evident what everyone will say of her."

"Not when our Aunt Emily arrives to take charge of Senorita Malliende."

"*Aunt Truscott*! Good grief, Patrick, your attic's to let."

"You cannot doubt our aunt is a most respectable lady," the earl pointed out, looking amused.

"And overbearing to the greatest degree. If you're not enamored of the chit, why bring her all the way from Spain. It is devilishly difficult for a bachelor."

"I cannot deny that, but Senorita Malliende deserves an opportunity to become famous. She has no possible chance in Spain at present where it is all chaos and like to be so for a long time to come."

Felix nodded his understanding of the situation at last. "You may rely upon my discretion for as long as it is necessary."

"I knew I could rely upon you, Felix, just as I have always done. When you see her dance, you will be well pleased."

When Felix glanced upstairs again, he saw the Spanish woman standing there, gazing down on them and he made haste to leave his cousin's house.

Felix climbed up on the box of his phaeton and raised his hand in salute as he took up the ribbons. As he drove away, he reflected that his cousin had lost none of his ability to set the town on its ears, and he gave silent thanks that his own life was so uncomplicated.

Four

From the first moment guests began arriving for the rout at Sir Magnus and Lady Kingsland's Manchester Square house, Sophia looked out anxiously for sight of her future husband. Unlike so many of her acquaintances Sophia no longer found it necessary to speculate upon the number of gentlemen who would press their attention upon her, which she found a great relief. Being settled, she decided, was sublime.

When Felix arrived, she excused herself from the circle of friends and admirers in which she was conversing and pushed her way through the crowds to greet him. As they made their way toward each other, Sophia could not help but reflect how handsome he was. He was not overly tall, but he certainly towered over her. His dark hair was fashionably cropped and his clothes of the latest style, although more extreme than Beau Brummell decreed to his followers, of which there were many.

Felix, when he reached her somewhere in the middle of the room, immediately raised her hand to his lips. "You look ravishing this evening, Sophia," he whispered so that only she could hear.

Her cheeks dimpled with pleasure. Her gown was of pink sarsnet with silver spangles which was a color she knew became her very well. Sophia was aware she looked her best, as indeed she should. In becoming betrothed to the heir of a viscount, she had achieved in a matter of weeks what other debutantes could not in an entire Season. Life could not be better.

"Thank you, Felix. It is kind of you to say so."

"If I cannot compliment my bride-to-be, who else may I favor? It is naught but the truth and I am persuaded many others have already echoed my thoughts this evening."

"As you know full well it is only your thoughts that matter to me, Felix."

"That is certainly what I hope is so."

"Isn't this the most delightful hurricane?"

"Only because you are present, my dear."

She laughed, tapping him teasingly on the arm with her fan. "Of course I am, dearest. This is my home."

"Not for much longer. Soon we shall have our own establishment, and that day cannot come soon enough for me."

They laughed together for a few minutes until the sound of the band striking up prompted Mr. Harcourt to say, "Dare I hope you have reserved this set for me?"

Again she laughed. "You know full well that I have—and many others. I may not wish to stand up with anyone other than you, but in all truth, Felix, since our betrothal, I am not as much in demand as I was before."

"That makes me happy even if it saddens a score of other gentlemen. I still marvel at my good fortune in winning your heart."

Sophia hid her pink cheeks behind her fan. "I fancy we are equal in our good fortune. You may not have heard but Captain Murchison has come up to scratch so it is now Celia's turn to cry roast meat this evening."

"I wish them both happy," the young man responded as the dance began, "but I do not envy him in becoming leg-shackled to such a hoyden."

They were both slightly breathless when the cotillion ended and it was then that Sophia noticed her future husband seemed slightly ill at ease as he glanced at frequent intervals toward the entrance.

"Felix, dear, is something amiss?" she inquired.

He assured her quite heartily. "By no means. I am naturally in great heart. How could I be any other?"

"Well, you did call upon Lord Manville yesterday and I did wonder if you had found him in a dire situation owing to his injuries, which are reputed to be horrendous."

"He is in excellent health and spirits, I assure you. None better. I own I was most pleasantly surprised."

Sophia looked perplexed at this disclosure. "I am naturally relieved to hear you say so, but I had heard he was most grievously injured at Cuidad Rodrigo."

"He was. I can scarce believe his good fortune, but miraculously he has recovered to a remarkable degree."

"So it seems, for Mama received a note from him this morning, informing her of your invitation to the rout and accepting. That would not indicate too great a degree of disability."

"Ah yes." Again the young man looked a mite uncomfortable. "I am in such a fidge for you to make his acquaintance and I was persuaded Lady Kingsland would not take it amiss if my cousin was to attend tonight."

"On the contrary, Felix, Mama is highly delighted that Lord Manville has chosen to make his first public appearance at our rout, but I am puzzled somewhat. From all accounts your cousin is something of a cripple. Are you telling me that is not so?"

"You will be able to judge for yourself before the evening is over," he told her maddeningly.

He began to lead her through the crowds then, saying, "Let us go to the conservatory where we can speak with more ease. I am making myself hoarse so you can hear me and everyone is hanging onto my every word. It is not to be borne."

Near the door they passed Jessica, who was almost surrounded by a group of callow young men. She waved impudently as the couple passed by, evidently enjoying the attention she was receiving.

"I do not envy the gentleman of her choice," Felix commented, an observation which made Sophia laugh.

"I really should give you a trimming, Felix," she scolded when at last they reached the quiet and solitude of the conservatory.

"I cannot conceive why. Surely not because I cried off to visit Manville yesterday. I was persuaded you would understand."

"Oh, indeed I did, but Celia called in and it seems, now he has returned, your cousin is the object of every *on-dit* in town and always was before he went away. I had no notion and I would very much like to know why you have spoken so little of him save to express your admiration of which he has only very recently become worthy."

Felix Harcourt smiled. "Since I met you, Sophia, my cousin has been the last person on my mind. My sole purpose, whenever we have had the good fortune to be together, has been to get to know *you*." He smiled wryly. "In any event, any recollection of his youthful exploits was not like to advance my suit."

Sophia's face relaxed into a smile once again. "As if I would blame you for another's scapegrace antics. You are nothing like your cousin if all I have heard is true."

"Quite so, not that I would for anything have you believe ill of him, for in truth he is a most splendid fellow."

Sophia cast him a wry look as they began to walk back toward the ballroom. "Felix, your loyalty does you great credit, but I have heard too many alarming tales about Lord Manville. Poor Lord Smythe lost an arm in a duel with your cousin and I am given to believe he was not the only gentleman to face Lord Manville's dueling pistols."

"*Poor* Lord Smythe," Felix mocked, "accused Manville of cheating at hazard. What is a fellow to do in those circumstances? What would any man of honor do?"

"Nevertheless I'm persuaded there are going to be a great many *on-dits* for the tattle-baskets to convey about him now that he is back."

Recalling the exquisite Spanish dancer he had seen in his cousin's house, Felix could not deny what Sophia said. He had given his word not to mention the woman to anyone, so he could not tell her, but he could well imagine the reaction of the rest of the beau monde when all was made public at last.

All at once he felt angry and wished his cousin had not come back to London at this very moment when he, Felix, was enjoying the happiest time of his life. Immediately the thought had come into his head, the young man regretted his resentment. He had never harbored such thoughts toward his cousin in his life before and couldn't understand why he should do so now after the earl had suffered so much in the Peninsula.

"Is he quite fully recovered?" Sophia was asking. "Or is it merely a matter of not being as bad as everyone believed?"

"I should say he is fully recovered, quite amazingly so. However, I do not think him *quite* the man he was, which is not so surprising. It is not, I feel, a physical thing. Well, in all truth, Sophia, he was never as bad as everyone believed, just a trifle wild, which is a fault in many young men."

"That does not excuse rakish behavior taken to

extremes," Sophia answered, casting him a wry glance.

"I daresay I am far too prejudiced to judge him properly. It is true he gambled to excess, drove recklessly." Felix laughed. "There is nothing odd about that. I recall when he was at Oxford he tipped the driver of the London stage a vail so he could drive the coach all the way up to London. And he did! I tell you, Sophia, it had to take a cannonball to unseat him. Nothing else ever could! He is a true Corinthian."

"What of Lady Whitchurch? I believe she cried off their betrothal when Lord Manville was so badly hurt in battle."

"I don't know the truth of the matter, but being acquainted with Manville, I believe it likely he wrote to her to tell her to cry off because he believed he would be an invalid for the rest of his life. His manservant told me—not Patrick you understand—he was obliged to teach himself to walk again. It was a long and painful business you may be sure."

Sophia gasped, her eyes wide. "I am full of admiration."

"So am I, and as for Lady Merinda Whitchurch, I know it would have seemed an excellent match between the two families, but I am of the firm opinion Manville never cared twopence for any female and in all truth, my dear, I don't suppose he ever will. For that, and that alone, I am inclined to pity him."

"I wonder why he is so lacking in feeling," Sophia mused.

"His mother was one of the great beauties of her

day. He never recovered from her death, which was, in my opinion, the source of his wild ways. He will never find a female to equal her in his eyes."

"I don't know whether I am in a fidge to meet him or in dread of it!"

"I would want you to like him. In all truth, dearest, I have met few females who did not. However, in your instance I am in two minds . . ."

His voice died away as they entered the ballroom. There in the middle of the room was a great crowd of people gathered in one place and there was about them a great air of excitement.

"It would appear that my cousin has arrived at last," Felix said with a crooked smile. "He is, I know, in a fidge to make your acquaintance, but it is as well to wait until some of the interest dies down—if indeed it does," he added with a laugh.

"He has caused more attention than Mr. Brummell did at Lady Cawthorne's ball," Sophia said in some surprise.

"It is to be hoped Boney does not surrender in the next sennight."

"Why on earth not?" Sophia asked, dragging her gaze away from the knot of people in the middle of the room.

"No one will take note of it while Manville's arrival in town remains a novelty."

Sophia and Felix were still laughing together when an imperious voice called, "Harcourt! Harcourt! There you are at last. Where have you been hiding yourself? I have been seeking you out for an age."

The young couple turned on their heels to find an imperious-looking lady approaching. She wore an

outmoded gown of puce velvet but she sported wonderful jewelry in every place possible to wear it,
and a confection of feathers in her hair that bobbed
with her every movement.

"Aunt Truscott," Felix said breathlessly, and he
looked ill at ease once more. Sophia had rarely seen
him as anxious as he had been for most of the evening. "Manville told me you were coming to stay,
but I had no notion you would be arriving so soon."

"When I received Manville's missive, I considered it a matter of urgency to get here as soon as I
was able."

She raised her quizzing glass and surveyed Sophia thoroughly. "This, I presume, is Miss Kingsland of whom I have heard a good deal of late."

Sophia dropped into a deep curtsy as Felix said,
still breathlessly, "Yes, Aunt, this is Sophia, my
bride-to-be. I am delighted to present to you my
aunt, Lady Truscott."

As Sophia straightened up again, she discovered
she was still being quizzed quite severely. However, a moment later Lady Truscott dropped her
quizzing glass and said in a warmer manner, "My
dear, I am bound to say my nephew has done well.
I did not expect him to display such good sense in
his choice of a bride."

Sophia blushed and Felix said wryly, "Thank you
for such confidence, Aunt."

"What has brought you up to town, Lady Truscott?" Sophia asked. "I have always been given to
understand that is a rare enough occurrence."

"He wishes that to be I do not doubt," the countess replied, casting her nephew a censorious look.

"By no means, Aunt . . ." Felix began to splutter.

"I deemed it wise to come up to town because Manville is just back from the war and Felix betrothed."

"You may be certain both Felix and I are delighted," Sophia assured her.

The countess smiled at last. "Why, thank you, my dear. How kind of you to say so."

"It is no more than the truth, Aunt," Felix added, a trifle tremulously.

"I have it in mind to remain for the rest of the Season," Lady Truscott informed them, "which will, naturally, take in your own wedding in due course." She glanced at Sophia momentarily before transferring her attention to the center of the room. "Manville is wasting no time in reacquainting himself with old friends. Let us hope on this occasion he will not be foolish enough to ally himself to a silly chit." When Sophia turned around, she noted that Lady Truscott was pointedly referring to Lady Whitchurch, who was standing close by. A moment later she addressed Sophia again. "Why do you not call in tomorrow at Park Lane where we will be able to engage in a coze with no interruptions?"

For a moment Sophia was slightly taken aback, but then, glancing uncertainly at Felix, she answered, "Thank you, Lady Truscott. I am honored by the invitation."

A moment later the countess hailed a friend and was gone. Felix let out a long breath and said, "My aunt is a formidable lady with definite opinions as you may have gathered, but she likes you, that much is evident."

"That is a great relief to me. I should have hated her to have taken me in dislike."

"As if anyone could," Felix chided, but it was evident he was greatly relieved.

"I was quaking at the thought of making her acquaintance, Felix, and I am so glad it is done. I have heard talk of Lady Truscott as a toplofty grande dame."

"She is," Felix answered wryly.

"Why did you not warn me she was coming to town? I could have prepared myself the better."

"I didn't know until Manville informed me of it yesterday, and even then I was not aware her arrival was imminent. I was never more shocked, I assure you," he added truthfully.

"From all you have told me about your cousin, I should not have thought he would welcome Lady Truscott as a guest in his home. It would surely be restricting to him."

Felix could not help but feel a little foolish. "I am given to understand Aunt Truscott will only reside at Park Lane for a short while."

"Even so . . ."

"It may seem a little odd for you to comprehend, dearest, but Manville and Lady Truscott have always enjoyed an excellent relationship. Lady Truscott has, to be plain, always doted upon Manville, which is a puzzle to us all. Without a doubt he is her favorite in the family."

Sophia gasped with annoyance. "That is so unfair, Felix! You are so good and kind . . ."

The young man looked down at her lovingly just as Jessica came rushing up to them. "Oh Sophia, Felix, is not Lord Manville utterly divine! I believe I am in love at last!"

Neither of them were given any chance to vent

their astonishment before one of Jessica's friends drew her away, the both of them laughing and chattering in earnest, no doubt about their meeting with the legendary Earl of Manville.

"Your cousin has found one female to champion his cause, even though she is a trifle young for him."

One of Mr. Harcourt's eyebrows rose a little. "I cannot vouch for that. He never used to be particular about the age of any female he encountered."

Sophia had no time to look alarmed before she caught sight of her mother pressing through the crowds, a smile on her lips and her cheeks unusually pink.

"We shall not be obliged to push our way through the crowds for you to meet my cousin," Felix said, glancing at Sophia. "Lady Kingsland is bringing him to us."

Suddenly Sophia was aware that her mother had her arm on that of one of the guests. She could see the top of a head of glossy Brutus-style hair, but because he was stopped at every turn, their progress was exceedingly slow and he was constantly surrounded by one group of people or another.

Naturally Sophia had assumed that Felix's nonesuch cousin used to be extremely stylish, but for so long she had imagined him an invalid covered in shawls, she knew now she would be obliged to alter her opinion of him to suit the new reality.

All at once the crowds parted nearby. Countless pairs of eyes surveyed the man who had come back from the dead. There were many whispers behind open fans. Sophia drew her attention from one of her friends who was engaging her in brief conversation and glanced at Felix, who was smiling and looking toward his cousin.

A moment later Sophia followed the direction of his gaze. She took in the dark blue evening coat sitting on broad shoulders, the black breeches fitted to perfection. Her gaze wandered up to the perfect folds of his neck cloth, fastened with a large diamond pin. His lips were already formed into the semblance of a welcoming smile, but most of all Sophia noted the dark eyes surveying her with what she took to be amusement. She had seen that look before, and those smiling lips were more than a little familiar to her.

All at once her head began to swim. She felt the room swirl around her. It couldn't be, she told herself sternly. It had to be her fanciful mind playing cruel tricks upon her. Felix's nonesuch cousin could not possibly be the shabby creature who had used her so abominably in Leeke Lane. No, it could not be. It was evident her nerves had been more affected by the incident than she believed, although she had never considered herself in the least vaporish before.

All at once a great stubbornness of will came to the fore and Sophia was determined not to swoon. She could not abide the questioning if she did, even though the room was insufferably hot and in such circumstances females often succumbed to the vapors. Indeed, it was not unknown for gentlemen to swoon in crowded rooms. Sophia, however, willed herself to remain calm and behave as if this was their very first meeting.

She opened her fan with one flick of her trembling hand and began to swish it to and fro with a

51

vengeance just as her mother crooned, "Sophia, dear, do allow me to present Lord Manville to you. He has been most anxious to make your acquaintance since he arrived."

The earl took Sophia's hand and raised it to his lips, but his eyes never left her face. "Your portrait does not do you justice, ma'am."

The moment he spoke, she was left in doubt no longer. This was he, but it still seemed impossible. Why had he been dressed so shabbily when it was evident he possessed the most elegant sartorial taste?

To cover her confusion, she sank into a deep curtsy even though her knees were very unsteady, and when she rose, she forced herself to meet his eyes, which she noted were still filled with that now familiar mockery.

The fan fluttered frantically in front of her pink cheeks. So many eyes were upon them it would be unbearable if he chose to divulge their previous encounter in so public a place.

"You flatter me, my lord," she managed to reply, aware of the acute interest of all those close by.

"My cousin sang your praises long and loud, Miss Kingsland, but not even he could do justice to the reality. He declares he is the most fortunate of men and I do not now doubt the truth of his statement."

His fulsome praise meant nothing to her, but at least she felt she could relax a little. If he had not at once declared their previous meeting, it surely meant he would not now do so in public. In any event Sophia told herself, she, at least, had done nothing of which she should be ashamed. It was he who had behaved in such an abominable manner and even with his formidable reputation as a rake, he would not wish to cry roast meat over it.

Consequently Sophia stood proud and looked him in the eye at last. "Felix warned me of your habit of speaking moonshine to ladies, my lord. You are, I fear, practiced in the art."

The earl laughed and Felix said, "Don't think Sophia is not up to snuff, Manville, 'cause I assure you she is."

"I am persuaded Miss Kingsland is quite an exceptional young lady." As her cheeks took on a deeper tinge of pink, the earl went on quickly, asking, "Now I am returned to London, I have great hopes of getting to know you the better. Dare I hope you have one set free to stand up with me this evening so we may make a start?"

Sophia was just about to answer in all truthfulness that she was engaged for every dance when Felix, to her utter chagrin replied, "Sophia and I are engaged to stand up for the quadrille together, but I am man enough to surrender her to you just on this one occasion, you understand."

Sophia shot him a furious look, which she was certain was intercepted by the earl even if it was not understood by Felix.

However, Lord Manville did not cry off, but bowed, saying, "Felix, your generosity toward me has never been more appreciated than now. Miss Kingsland?"

Sophia could see quite clearly she had no choice but to allow him to lead her onto the dance floor where others were assembling for the quadrille. It was no consolation that Felix followed with her mother on his arm and they both looked in high spirits. Sophia was not much impressed by the fact she was the most envied female in the room. Being in the same building as Lord Manville only served to mortify her, dancing with him caused her extreme anguish. However, it was some solace to her that no one present could possibly imagine the depths of her emotions just then.

"I do hope Lady Kingsland is enjoying *Pride and Prejudice*," he ventured as they took their place in the set.

Sophia's cheeks flamed once again at the reminder of their last encounter and she replied tartly, "Yes, I thank you, but I do wonder if you have made the inquiry of her."

"No, ma'am. It is evident no one knows of our previous meeting. Indeed, why should they? The tattle-baskets will be better pleased with the tale of a mysterious stranger who came to your rescue, and I am in no fidge for anyone to know I behaved in so shabby a manner before I left you. When we had our . . . er encounter I had just returned to town and had not visited either my barber or my tailor. Happily those omissions have now been rectified."

"In all truth, my lord, I had not noticed," she told him as the music began and to her relief she was not obliged to converse with him any further.

Once the dance was over, he began to escort her back to the edge of the floor, only to find their way, in a manner, barred. The earl's expression did not alter—Sophia was bound to admire his inscrutability at that moment—as Lady Whitchurch stood before them.

Several Seasons ago, as a debutante, Merinda Daley had been the rage of the *ton*. Her face and fortune had brought gentlemen to her door in scores. No one was surprised, however, when she accepted an offer of marriage from Lord Manville, who was considered to be one of the most eligible bachelors.

It was generally acknowledged that they were well suited, for if anyone could curb his rakish ways, the delectable Merinda Daley could. Sophia did not doubt that at that very moment there were those setting wagers on the inevitability of them once again forming a very close friendship.

"My lady," he greeted her with only the briefest inclination of his head.

Just at that moment Sophia wondered the truth of what Felix had told her. Had Lord Manville cried off their betrothal or had it been, as was generally believed, Lady Whitchurch, afraid she might be forced to marry a helpless invalid? Sagely Sophia doubted if anyone would ever know the truth of the matter. It was of no more account, for shortly afterward Merinda Daley had married the Marquis of Whitchurch, who had adored her from the time of her come out.

"I was told you were back in town," the marchioness said with no pause for niceties.

"On this particular occasion your information was correct, ma'am," he replied, his voice heavy with irony.

It gave Sophia some strange satisfaction to note that he did not linger over Lady Whitchurch's hand.

"I am pleased to see you looking in such rude health, Manville," she persisted.

"I confess I have never been better, and I am

bound to say you have never looked lovelier, my lady."

The woman smiled with satisfaction as Felix came to join them. He looked rather anxious. Then the earl nodded to Sophia and to Lady Whitchurch before striding off in the direction of the card room. As she watched him go, Lady Whitchurch continued to smile, evidently satisfied with their initial meeting while all around voices buzzed, having witnessed the most interesting confrontation in an age.

"That could have been a deucedly awkward moment," Felix confided in a low voice.

"I am not entirely certain that it was not," Sophia responded.

"My dance, I believe," Felix said, drawing a deep sigh as the music started up again.

Reluctantly Sophia allowed him to lead her onto the dance floor, but it was patently evident that Lord Manville's return to London was the precursor of an interesting Season. The only pity was she did not feel far enough removed to sit back and enjoy it as so many others were preparing to do.

Five

Fearful of being late for her call upon Lady Truscott, Sophia arrived early at Lord Manville's house in Park Lane the following day.

She was sitting in her carriage, wondering what she should do to pass the time, and even though it was unusual for a gentleman to be at home at that time of the day, all at once she was fearful of encountering the earl himself. As she sat in the carriage deep in thought, her attention was attracted by someone calling to her from outside the railings.

Sophia immediately climbed down from the carriage and walked across to speak to Celia Waddell who was accompanying Captain Murchison in his cabriolet.

"Good day to you, Miss Kingsland," the young man greeted her with a smile, raising his high-crowned beaver hat.

"Good day, Captain Murchison," Sophia responded, and noted that Celia looked excited as she glanced toward Manville House before returning her attention to her friend.

"I did not look to see you *here*, Sophia," she told her, her eyes bright with speculation.

Her friend cast her a wry look. "You should not be at all surprised, for I am engaged to call upon Lady Truscott, Mr. Harcourt's aunt, who is lately come to town."

Celia appeared disappointed by so prosaic an explanation. "Oh, indeed. I had quite forgotten he and Lord Manville are cousins and that Lady Truscott is their aunt."

Sophia smiled sweetly. "I am persuaded you must have made acquaintance with Lord Manville last night, Celia."

Once again Miss Waddell's eyes became bright. "I did, indeed. He was utterly charming to me, I own, and will cause a deal of excitement now he is returned."

"I have warned Miss Waddell not to allow herself to be taken in by his moonshine," Captain Murchison broke in, laughing uncomfortably. "There are some of us who recall that Manville is quite a dangerous man where females are concerned. I doubt if the rake is reformed."

"Oh, faddle!" his bride-to-be complained. "I am no green girl to be taken in by his flummery, although I am bound to own he is most pleasant."

"Well," Sophia said briskly, "it is his aunt I am engaged to call upon. Lady Truscott had been exceedingly condescending to me, I own."

"It was noted that his lordship danced only with you last night," Celia went on to her friend's annoyance. "What a singular honor for you. I'm persuaded most of those females present last night longed to stand up with him, myself included!" she added, laughing coyly as she cast a sly glance at Captain Murchison.

"My dear," he answered in the ironic tone so fashionable among gentlemen at present, "no young lady should aspire to partner Manville. His predilection for all manner of vices is well-known."

Celia frowned and Sophia said quickly, "No doubt, as I have just become betrothed to his cousin, he deemed it appropriate to stand up with me above all others. And recall, he is not long from his sickbed and mayhap he did not feel robust enough to stand up for more than the one set."

The young lady's eyebrows rose a fraction as she considered the possibility. "He looked as fit as a flea to me, and he has taken pains to make it known that his recovery is complete."

"I would not doubt it for a moment," Sophia answered quickly, "but it is very possible his injured limbs still ache, especially during a hectic dance."

"Very like," Celia agreed at last, much to Sophia's relief, although why she was troubling to make such excuses on Lord Manville's behalf, she had no notion.

Celia Waddell took the ribbons from Captain Murchison and as he raised his hat in Sophia's direction, once again the cabriolet set off down Park Lane.

At the very same time Sophia was in a quake over her prospective visit to Lady Truscott, in a house nearby Lady Whitchurch was pacing the floor of her elegant drawing room, deep in thought.

When she heard a carriage stop outside, she hurried across to the window and peered down into the street to see Lord Manville alighting from his elegant curricle. When, a few minutes later, he was ushered into the drawing room, it was to find the marchioness reclining on a daybed, a copy of *The Ladies' Magazine* on her lap, a box of marchpane on a table by her side.

"Ah, Manville, how good of you to come," she greeted him, offering one long, slim hand.

He bent briefly over her hand. "I came in response to your note, my lady, as soon as I was able."

When he withdrew to take a seat some distance from her, she cast him a coy look. "You have become cruel in your absence, Manville."

"I scarcely think I can be credited with more cruelty than used to be."

"Once I would not have had to summon you."

He smiled slightly. "I would not for anything cause you any distress, my lady, so let me beg your pardon most heartily for the omission."

"I do fear you are roasting me, Manville, but I shall chastise you no longer," she replied, not missing the heavily ironic tone of his voice. "I sent for you to call only so we could have a long-overdue coze away from the eyes of those who would make much of it."

The earl's eyebrows rose slightly and he paused to take a pinch of snuff, all the while observing his onetime betrothed. "I am bound to own that the years have dealt kindly with you, Merinda."

She beamed. "And with you, Patrick, which is

especially remarkable after all you have been obliged to endure since leaving England." Her smile faded somewhat then. "I do believe you are entitled to an explanation of my conduct over our betrothal."

"I don't consider it relevant any longer," he told her and there was no mistaking the boredom that had crept into his voice.

Lady Whitchurch sat up straight, disregarding the magazine she had draped so carefully across her lap. "It is exceedingly relevant to me, for I don't wish to be at dagger's drawn with you."

"You may rest assured I bear you no ill will, my dear."

The marchioness continued to look anxious. "That is a great relief to me, for I can assure you now I truly wished to be your bride, only it was said you had been given notice to quit and I was so wretched at the thought of losing you. I truly did not know what to do, and Whitchurch was so attentive to me."

The earl smiled. "I recall he always was."

"So you do understand my dilemma?"

"Perfectly."

She looked, for a moment, petulant. "There was a time when you would have taken it amiss that I became leg-shackled to one of your cronies."

The earl waved one hand in the air dismissively. "Oh, I believe you to be most admirably suited with Whitchurch, my dear."

"So you truly do not mind that I wed another?"

"Have I not already told you so?" A moment later he went on, "Merinda, the truth is, I was always aware you were worthy of better than I."

A look of satisfaction came over her face at last. "I cannot tell you how relieved I am at your attitude, Patrick."

"I am not the unfeeling brute some would have you believe, and your very evident marital bliss is a great pleasure for me to observe."

Once again the marchioness looked uncertain in the face of this admission. "My one great fear, once I heard you were about to return to London, was that, mayhap, you might call out poor Whitchurch . . ."

The earl laughed. "What a crack-brained notion!"

"Nevertheless it was a great fear to me. You were always known for hotheaded pursuit when your pride was injured, and you have called men out for much, much less."

He took out his gold hunter and glanced at it before returning it to his pocket. "You may rest assured, Merinda, you need have no fear for your spouse." He got to his feet, towering over her. "And now I regret I must leave you for a rather pressing engagement."

"You are so much in demand," she said coquettishly, "I am honored you have found this time for me."

"I hope I shall always have time for you, my dear," he assured her as she escorted him toward the door.

"We were once very close, Patrick," she said, touching him lightly on the arm. "It would please me if we could resume a close friendship once again."

He subjected her to one of his inscrutable stares

before he answered, "That is a most civilized suggestion, Merinda. Good day."

After he had gone, Lady Whitchurch smiled to herself, confident that the meeting had gone extremely well, but she could not be certain. She had little time to reflect upon the matter before Lord Pinkton was ushered in, and she greeted him with rather less enthusiasm than he had been accustomed to receiving.

A few minutes after bidding her friend good-bye, Sophia, wearing her newest blue velvet pelisse, was ushered into Lady Truscott's neat drawing room.

The room was, in fact, as large as many a grand drawing room she had visited and was filled with elegant French furniture, the floor covered by Aubusson rugs. The house had evidently been built with large families in mind, but as Lord Manville had only the one sister who was now married and lived quietly in the country, the house was evidently far too big for a bachelor. It was evident that Lady Truscott could live quite comfortably in several rooms without ever encountering her nephew if she so wished.

Manville House was an enormous pile, built, Felix had told her, as a fitting showpiece for Lord Manville's late mother, who was a great beauty and loved entertaining on a lavish scale. Unfortunately she had died very soon after the house had been completed, leaving the late earl adrift and unable to control his willful son.

Wearing brown kerseymere and a lace cap, Lady Truscott came forward to greet her guest in the warmest of tones. "Miss Kingsland, my dear, how good it is to see you again. Tea will be served presently, but in the meantime do sit down."

Accustomed to mixing with the highest-placed people in the land, Sophia could not help but find Lady Truscott daunting, and she felt decidedly ill at ease, which perhaps also owed something to her fear of encountering Lord Manville himself.

As she seated herself on a brocade sofa near the fire and drew off her gloves, she could not help but be aware of the portrait over the mantel of the late Lady Manville, in her youth, painted by Thomas Gainsborough. Her beauty had not been overstated by Felix, although Sophia could not detect any likeness to her son in her appearance. Lady Manville had been as fair as her son was dark.

Lady Truscott noted Sophia's interest in the portrait and said, "Her presence is still sorely missed by the entire family."

"I can understand that, my lady."

"Laura was the one true beauty in the family." She laughed deprecatingly. "No one could understand from whom it came. Our family was never famed for its looks."

"You do yourself an injustice, my lady," Sophia felt bound to say.

"You are very kind to say so, my dear, but it is undoubtedly true. You may have noted that both Manville and Felix favor their fathers who were, most fortunately, rather handsome in their youth. Felix's mother and I were the plain ones, although we did well enough for all that, I own. Unfortunately both my sisters were consumptive, whereas I have always been as strong as an ox." Her eyes narrowed suddenly. "I do trust that you have a strong constitution, my dear."

"Indeed," Sophia answered with a nervous laugh.

"Good. Good. It is hoped, if you will forgive my being indelicate, that you and dear Felix will fill a large nursery before too long." Sophia found her cheeks growing pink. "After all, the family is not strong on progeny," Lady Truscott added with a laugh. "I have lost all hope of Manville becoming leg-shackled."

Sophia sat very stiffly, clutching her reticule. She was in a way outraged until she recalled that Lady Truscott was the product of an earlier, more earthy age.

"I regret you will be obliged to wait a while, my lady, for Felix and I do not plan to be married until the summer."

"Although I could not be more delighted at this alliance—I am well acquainted with your family, my dear—you are both a mite young to form a firm commitment, so the small delay is sensible."

"We are no younger than many others who become betrothed," Sophia pointed out.

"No, indeed, and I can perceive that you are the most sensible *jeune fille* it was possible for my nephew to choose, but Felix is a trifle immature. Not that it signifies and I confess I had not thought of it myself until Manville made mention of his doubts on the matter. I was bound to agree with much of what he said. Marriage is a very serious matter."

Sophia's eyes grew wide. "Lord Manville? What has the matter of our marriage to do with Lord Manville, ma'am?"

Lady Truscott smiled rather foolishly, which irritated Sophia all the more. "Nothing save for the fact Manville has always had an avuncular interest in Felix. They have always been much closer than others of a similar relationship."

"I had noted it," Sophia answered, "but they are not in the least alike, which makes such a friendship odd."

"I could not agree with you more. It has always been a great puzzle to me. When Felix was very young it was regrettable that he looked to Manville so much. He regarded him as a hero when he was no such thing. A scapegrace more like. With very good reason the family feared that Manville would seduce Felix into bad ways, but to his credit he did not, and Felix continued to admire his cousin regardless of his behavior, which was not always as it ought to be. However, I am bound to admit that there is much to admire in him nowadays."

Sophia found herself unable to concur. "So it is Lord Manville who considers Felix too young to marry."

"Do not take it amiss, my dear. It was foolish of me to have mentioned the matter. I have become a trifle addlepated in my old age. I have no doubt at all Manville will be proved wrong in due course."

"Indeed he will," Sophia affirmed, her cheeks pink.

Lady Truscott rose from her seat to pull the bellpull that hung at the side of the mantel. When she returned to sit opposite her guest, she said, "I intend to give you a pearl diadem to mark the occasion of your betrothal to my nephew."

All at once Sophia's outrage was gone and she

gasped. "Lady Truscott, that is far too generous of you."

The countess held up her hand to forestall any further protest. "I had always intended to share my jewels between Felix's wife and Manville's. I now have no doubt that most of it will come to you in time . . ."

"Not for a long time, I trust, my lady."

The woman smiled. "In any event Manville has most of his mother's fabulous jewel collection in the unlikely event he does become leg-shackled. I do not envy any female he is like to wed. I am afraid his fearsome reputation is not like to endear him to any likely bride."

"He was once betrothed—to Lady Whitchurch."

"Oh that goosecap. She did him a great service in crying off."

Sophia smiled wryly. "I doubt if Lord Manville shares your feelings on the matter."

"He will if he possesses the good sense I perceive in him."

"What of Lord Manville's sister?" Sophia asked, anxious to learn more about other members of the family of which she would soon become a part.

"Julia is as odd as he was used to be. Neither the Manville jewels nor my own would sit upon her comfortably."

"Oh . . . ?" Sophia looked intrigued.

"Oh, 'tis nothing sinister, I assure you," Lady Truscott responded to Sophia's curiosity. "Julia, you see, requires no finery living as she does so deep in the country. She wishes for nothing more."

"It seems to me from what you say, ma'am, she is quite unlike her brother."

"That is true, but they do have an affinity. It was to Julia, Manville went directly on his return from the Peninsula. It was in her capable hands he was returned to full health. Ah, here is tea."

Several servants arrived bearing silver salvers. A teakettle occupied one salver and fine Derby china another. Served with the tea was an assortment of biscuits and delicious cake.

When Lady Truscott poured the tea, a footman brought the cup to Sophia while another offered her biscuits and cake. When Sophia noted that she was pouring tea into a third cup, she feared the worst. The nephew on whom Lady Truscott obviously doted was about to join them.

Before any explanation could be made, a soft knock on the door heralded the arrival of a young lady whom Sophia judged to be only a little older than herself. She was small and slim, and extremely dark in coloring, so much so she wondered briefly if this might be Lord Manville's sister, Julia, who thought so little of the Social Season she could not be prized away from her horses or her estate in Yorkshire.

"Do come in Manuela," Lady Truscott urged when the girl seemed to hesitate by the door. "I would like you to meet Miss Kingsland, who is soon to marry my other nephew, Mr. Felix Harcourt."

The young lady curtsied briefly while considering Sophia very carefully indeed. "Miss Kingsland, I am honored to make your acquaintance."

Her English was spoken carefully with a heavy accent that some might find attractive. In fact, Sophia was bound to admit to herself that it was attractive.

The countess looked up from her pouring of the tea to explain, "This is Senorita Malliende. She is Manville's new protégée."

Sophia's eyes grew wide with disbelief. Surely Lady Truscott could not be so ingenuous or even adoring of her nephew to believe such a thing. Sophia was far too sophisticated to betray any shock, but *protégée*? She had to struggle very hard not to laugh out loud at such a ludicrous notion.

Manuela Malliende sat down with her dainty cup of tea. Even though Sophia herself was small and slim, this woman made her feel like an overweight matron of the *ton*. To give the earl his due, his taste could not be in doubt. He always seemed to choose the most beautiful ladies as a companion, from Lady Whitchurch to Manuela Malliende.

"Senorita Malliende comes from Spain," Lady Truscott explained, rather unnecessarily Sophia thought.

However, she smiled over the rim of her cup, aware that Senorita Malliende still continued to examine her and there was something extremely discomforting about the scrutiny.

"Senorita Malliende is a dancer," Lady Truscott went on, smilingly.

"That is most interesting," Sophia answered, putting down her cup.

She really didn't know how to react to Senorita Malliende, but she guessed her friend, Celia Waddell, would have given her finest lace fan to be the first to know of this matter. How characteristic of the outrageous earl that he had no intention of hiding her away. No doubt he had every reason to be proud of his latest *chère amie*, especially as everyone had put him down as a hopeless invalid after his future bride had married another. How it was going to amuse him when he finally presented her to the *ton* with the approval of his most respectable aunt. Sophia was bound to admire his audacity, if not his morals.

"His lordship has a great deal of faith in me," the girl said deprecatingly. "I am not so sure I am as good as he believes, and in all truth I would not wish to disappoint him."

"Everyone will be able to judge for themselves on Friday evening," the countess told her, and the young lady laughed uncertainly again.

"I am in a quake whenever I think on it, you may be sure."

"You will be a triumph," Lady Truscott assured her.

"So his lordship keeps telling me. After Friday he says I shall be the rage of the *ton*, but I cannot conceive it is possible."

Her laugh was like the tinkling of a silver bell, and it irritated Sophia greatly.

"Your English is excellent, senorita," she ventured, unable to rid her voice of its icy tone.

"His lordship was very patient when he taught me. I am, as yet, far from perfect, but I do try, and I aim to improve in time." She eyed Sophia with interest once again. "So it is you who is to marry Mr. Harcourt."

Sophia was somewhat miffed to discover that the earl must have discussed her affairs with this opera-dancer, and her tone remained cool. "You are correct, senorita."

"I am bound to say I regard you as the most fortunate female, ma'am. Mr. Harcourt is a very fine gentleman."

Again Sophia's eyes grew wide. "Are you acquainted with Fe . . . Mr. Harcourt?"

Manuela Malliende's eyes sparkled. "Not acquainted exactly, ma'am, but we have met briefly."

"He did not tell me of it!"

The Spanish woman continued to smile, not at all put out by Sophia's evident dismay. "No doubt he considered it a matter of so little import."

At that statement Sophia's lip began to curl, although she really could not credit her own outrage. If the earl wished to bring his *chère amie* from Spain and install her in his house with his toplofty aunt as chaperon, it was of no concern to her. Nor was a brief meeting with Felix anything to put her out of countenance, but there was no doubt that it did. Sophia was both surprised and disgusted with herself for these unsophisticated feelings.

With undue haste she began to gather up her gloves and reticule. "I regret to leave so soon, but I must, my lady."

"No doubt you have a deal to do, my dear, but we shall most certainly meet again before long."

"I look forward to that, too," Senorita Malliende said. "I have as yet no friends in England. Mayhap, when I need advice on matters which are strange to me, I may come to you, Miss Kingsland."

Sophia smiled frostily, not in the least flattered. "I can assure you, Lady Truscott is far more experienced in all matters you may need to consult upon than I can possibly be. Good day, ladies."

As the footman escorted her down the stairs, Sophia continued to fume in silence. It had been an

71

outrageous act when Lord Manville had assaulted her, but she could in some measure excuse him on the grounds he did not know her to be a lady. That, at least, would always remain a private matter between the two of them, irritating as it was to her memory, but she did not doubt he would continue to voice his fears about Felix's youth, which was only to mask his disapproval of her as his cousin's wife. Or, indeed, it might only be his wish always to be a prime mover in Felix's affairs. After all, Felix had had the temerity of offering for her without first consulting his cousin and gaining his approval. How that would gall the mighty Lord Manville! she fumed.

Now, in addition to these outrages against her, he seemed determined to pass off his Spanish doxy in the guise of respectability on the unsuspecting *ton*. Belatedly she could see why he was spoken of in such disparaging terms by those who had known him for some time. If he was not a rakehell, no other gentleman she could think of would meet the requirements. His ability to cause mischief had not been ended by his sojourn in the Peninsula. It was evident to Sophia he still possessed the desire to cause trouble and intended to do so whenever he was able.

Her carriage awaited her beneath the porte cochere. Unfortunately she had not managed to climb inside before the earl's curricle thundered into the courtyard and pulled up behind. Sophia had no choice but to delay her departure sufficiently to acknowledge his greeting, but she was in no mood to enjoy social intercourse with this man, toward whom she harbored a violent dislike.

"Miss Kingsland! What splendid good fortune to encounter you here!"

"Good day to you, my lord," she responded mutinously, her eyes sparkling with the fury she was obliged to suppress.

His eyes narrowed slightly when he became aware of the coolness in her manner. "I do trust you are in good health today, ma'am."

Sophia stiffened. "Indeed. I have never been more robust, my lord."

"I have only made mention of it because your cheeks appear to be a trifle flushed."

Now Sophia smiled with a sureness she did not feel. "Have no fear, I shall endeavor to use a little less rouge in future."

"I assure you it is most becoming." He paused for a moment before asking, "I do trust you enjoyed your coze with Aunt Emily."

"Very much. It was most informative, and I have naturally made the acquaintance of Senorita Malliende. You are to be congratulated; she is quite delightful."

"I could not agree with you more, Miss Kingsland. However, her charm is nothing compared to her talent, which will burst upon the public at large like a shower of precious stones."

Sophia's lips curled into the semblance of a smile. "How poetic you are, my lord. I had not thought it in you."

"I am a man of great surprises, ma'am."

"I do not doubt it in the least."

"I do trust you will be among those present at Covent Garden on Friday evening."

"Oh indeed. I would not wish to miss it for anything."

"I am confident that Senorita Malliende has a dazzling future before her and the management of Covent Garden agree with me on that score."

When it appeared he was about to stand back to allow her to climb into the carriage, she couldn't stop herself saying, "It has come to my notice that you are concerned about Felix's fitness for marriage." He frowned and she went on, "To be frank, you consider him rather young to be embarking upon matrimony."

His face cleared. 'It is perfectly true that when I came to hear of his betrothal, I was troubled, fearing that he might have allied himself to some chit who has more hair than wit; but I can assure you, ma'am, since making your acquaintance, I have no doubts about the rightness of what he is doing."

"You relieve me, for I am fully aware of the store Felix puts upon everything you say and do."

He smiled deprecatingly. "You overestimate that, ma'am."

"I consider you are being too modest," she snapped, "but I am of the opinion that you do tend to overestimate your own wisdom. You may know a great deal about females in general, but nothing about ladies in particular, and in matters of the heart you really have no experience. Felix and I love each other. You must own, my lord, you can have no possible notion of *that* emotion."

So saying, she climbed into the carriage at last, but not before deriving some measure of satisfaction from the look of utter bleakness that had come into his eyes. There seemed no doubt that Lady

Whitchurch's marriage had affected him more than he would ever admit, and Sophia presumed this could well be another reason he wished to come between her and Felix. He was envious of their convivial relationship. While she could understand his feelings, she did, all the same, despise him for such shallowness.

When the carriage door was closed, he came to speak to her through the window. "Miss Kingsland, if you believe I would attempt to make Felix cry off, you could not be more wrong."

He raised his high-crowned beaver hat as the carriage set off and she sank back into the squabs. She was not proud of herself for betraying her anger or for the cruel reminder of his own faithless love. Whatever were his ambivalent feelings toward *her*, she suddenly felt she should not stoop to his level of heartlessness.

"His lordship does remind me of someone," Lily ventured, glancing out of the back window, "but I really cannot recall who it can be."

"No doubt it is Mr. Harcourt, as they are cousins," Sophia snapped. "There is some slight resemblance between them, if only one looks to see it."

When the carriage paused before entering Park Lane, she also glanced back to see him staring after them and she wondered why, despite his pledge of innocence, she felt no reassurance at all.

Six

As might have been expected, the opera house was packed to capacity the following Friday evening. The streets in the vicinity of Covent Garden had been choked with aristocratic carriages filled with bejeweled people, clad in their finest clothes, for some considerable time before the performance was due to begin. When the carriages finally arrived outside the porticoed entrance to the opera house, passengers were discharged to stream inside and mingle with those already arrived.

Sophia, wearing a gown of sarsnet and a circlet of pearls around her neck, watched the arrivals with keen interest. The pearl diadem promised to her by Lady Truscott had been delivered to Manchester Square by one of the countess's footmen, and Sophia wore it nestling in her fair curls.

Word of Manuela Malliende's debut had spread through the ranks of the *ton* like a fire out of control. Those who did not possess their own box and could not acquire a ticket to the pit, shamelessly sought a seat in the box of any acquaintance they could find.

"I trust that Senorita Malliende does not disappoint after all the fuss and botheration her appearance is causing," commented Lady Kingsland as their party assembled in the lobby of the theater.

"Do you doubt Lord Manville's taste, Mama?" Jessica asked pointedly. "I for one do not."

"I would not doubt his taste in females," Sir Magnus answered with a gruff laugh. "Of dancers I am not so sure."

"Really, dear," his wife admonished, "there is no need for such comments."

She glanced pointedly at their two daughters and Sir Magnus had the grace to look shamefaced. When a moment later Sir Magnus and Lady Kingsland wandered away to greet an old acquaintance, Sophia smilingly acknowledged several of her own.

"I, for one, believe Senorita Malliende will be superb tonight," Felix said, smiling broadly at the two young ladies.

Sophia's face took on a flinty look. "At what, may I ask?"

The young man looked bewildered. "At dancing, naturally. That is why she is here. Indeed, it is the reason Manville brought her all the way from Spain."

Jessica giggled behind her fan, causing her sister to cast her a dark look. "Of course, I had quite forgotten that you have had the singular privilege of meeting her."

"Only fleetingly, I regret to say."

His face grew rather red at the sight of his bride-to-be's cold look.

"Evidently you were highly impressed with the lady, but it could not have been her dancing that made you sensible of her qualities."

"You seem to have taken her in dislike, Sophia, and I cannot for anything conceive why."

"Tush! What a nonsense. She is perfectly amiable, I find. However, if she made such a great impression upon you, I can only wonder why. Nor can I conceive why you did not tell me you have met her, Felix."

"As I said, it was only a fleeting encounter and Manville asked for my discretion until she was properly settled."

"I do not wonder," Sophia murmured, swishing her fan to and fro, "seeing she was so cosily ensconced in his house in Park Lane."

"Now, now, Sophia, there is no need to infer what is not true. It is sufficient that others will do so."

"Do you wonder what everyone will think?" she asked airily, enjoying his discomfiture.

"I have it from Manville himself that it isn't so."

Sophia laughed. "Everyone knows he can lie faster than a dog can trot when it suits his purpose, and his reputation with the ladies has passed into legend."

"Sophia, I cannot hold with that. I have never known my coz to tell an untruth. It has never been one of his vices."

"If not," Sophia answered smilingly, "it must be one of the few."

Jessica laughed again. "Only think, Sophia, you will soon be related to him."

"I cannot conceive what has put you so out of humor, my dear," Felix told her. "If I did not know you better, I would suspect you were deliberately trying to provoke me."

"Stuff and nonsense!" she responded. "However, I do feel bound to say I take exception to your cousin interfering in our affairs, which you must own he has no right to do!"

The young man looked taken aback. "Manville? Interfering in our affairs? I cannot conceive what you may mean, Sophia. You do refer to Manville, I take it?"

Sophia continued to fan herself furiously. "Who else? You cannot deny he attempted to persuade you to cry off our marriage."

"I most certainly do deny it! Why, my coz has done nothing but sing your praises to me every time we meet. Why should he wish me to cry off?"

"On the face of it he believes you too young for matrimony."

"Sophia," he answered with a profound sigh, "I fear you have put the saddle on the wrong horse in this race. He is delighted by our match, none more so."

"Do you believe Lord Manville intends to settle down himself now he has returned to England?" Jessica asked, in an attempt to defuse what had become a highly charged situation.

"I cannot say," Felix answered shortly. "I suppose it is always possible, although not likely. Why do you ask?"

The girl looked coy as she fluttered her fan in front of her face. Sophia used hers to cool her hot cheeks.

"I am to come out next Season, and if he is available, he is the most eligible gentleman . . ."

"You are a goosecap," her sister told her, casting her a withering look. "As if Lord Manville would be interested in a green girl like you."

Hastily Felix said, looking somewhat relieved, "Here are Miss Waddell and Captain Murchison at last. I think it is time to go to our box. The performance will soon begin."

When Celia and Captain Murchison emerged through the crowds, Sophia was able to greet her friends with genuine warmth, but as the group made its way toward the box, she was shaken to realize she had almost quarreled with Felix for the very first time, and she knew exactly who was to blame for that. She and Felix had enjoyed a perfect understanding before the earl had returned to town. Everything that irked between them was concerned with Lord Manville.

By the time the Kingsland party became ensconced in the box, the expectant air in the theater was evident to all who were fortunate enough to be there. Scarcely a person of any consequence was absent, for although the main attraction of the evening was supposed to be *Semiramide*, in reality it was Manuela Malliende whom everyone wished to see.

The moment they were seated, Sophia quizzed the other boxes for a sight of the earl, for it was evident he would be present. She had found herself looking for him in the lobby, too. After their last encounter Sophia did not relish a meeting and she resolved once again to avoid him at all costs, however difficult that might prove to be.

"La! If that is not outside of enough!" Lady Kingsland exclaimed and all those in the box followed the direction in which she was looking.

Moments later it became quite evident why Lady Kingsland was so surprised. In one of the nearby boxes Lord Manville and Lady Truscott were taking their places alongside none other than Lord and Lady Whitchurch.

"Good grief!" Felix cried. "Who would have thought it possible?"

Lady Whitchurch was smiling and acknowledging the greetings of her acquaintances. It was apparent by her demeanor, she was fully aware of achieving quite a coup in having Lord Manville and his aunt in her box.

Her white muslin gown, in the latest style, was cunningly designed to show off her white shoulders and bosom to best effect. Acknowledged as a great beauty, Sophia grudgingly owned that Lady Whitchurch did throw a shadow over those who were more commonplace.

"How clever of Lord Manville," Celia declared. "His appearance in the box with Lady Whitchurch will no doubt prove he harbors no ill will toward her. It will still a great many tongues."

"Just as Senorita Malliende's appearance will make others clack," Jessica added.

"He cannot be accused of keeping both as his *chère amie*," Lady Kingsland pointed out, a statement that caused her husband to laugh uproariously.

"Do not lay any wagers upon it, my dear!"

"Whatever did we talk about when his lordship was in the Peninsula?" Captain Murchison asked.

"No one nearly as interesting," Celia answered.

The Whitchurch party including the earl, acknowledged the nods from Sir Magnus and Lady Kingsland's box until a moment later when the attention of all those present was diverted by the arrival of none other than the Prince Regent himself.

Wearing a splendid dress uniform and the garter star, he entered the Royal Box accompanied by Princess Charlotte and Lady Hertford, who was his current favorite. No doubt because of Princess Charlotte's presence, no one jeered the Prince, as had become normal practice whenever he appeared in public nowadays.

After the playing of the national anthem, the royal party was seated and the performance could begin at last. As was usual, starting was somewhat late.

As the lights went down, Sophia turned to cast Felix a smile, regretting her former waspishness. She knew full well that he was not to blame for her megrims and she determined not to allow the earl to drive a wedge of any kind between Felix and herself.

The performance of *Semiramide* should have been most enjoyable. In a way it was, and no less enjoyable than previous performances, but the audience was in a fidge to see Manuela Malliende and its impatience was very evident throughout the first half of the evening.

Sophia found herself hoping that the Spanish dancer would be a great disappointment to the assembled crowd, but somehow she doubted if it would be so. The thought depressed and alarmed her, for she had never harbored the slightest malice toward any other creature before and could not fathom why she should begin to do so now. Oddly enough she had gained the distinct impression that Senorita Malliende was equally reserved about her.

"It is quite like old times, don't you think?" Lady Whitchurch whispered to the earl as the theater became dark.

"Not quite, my dear," he replied, glancing at her mockingly. "You have become a married lady and I have seen a little of a very cruel world since the time to which you refer."

The marchioness was not at all put out by his words. She put her hand lightly on his arm and moved a little closer in the darkness. "No doubt any strangeness we feel in each other's presence will soon disappear and we will be able to enjoy each other's company even more than we did before."

The interval arrived after what seemed to be a very long time to the impatient audience. Most of those present filed out into the lobbies and corridors in search of refreshment, a drink, or simply to show off their magnificent apparel.

The atmosphere of anticipation had intensified and everyone was eager to talk of the treat to come. As Felix was one of the few who had actually met Senorita Malliende, he was only too eager to speak of the experience to anyone who would listen and there were many only too eager to hang on to his every word. Sophia soon grew weary of what she called Manuela-fever and wandered away in search of more conducive conversation on any other subject, if indeed it was at all possible.

At one point she almost came face-to-face with

the earl, but as he was intently in conversation with Lady Whitchurch, who appeared delighted to be in his company, Sophia had no difficulty in avoiding a meeting by turning on her heel and walking back the way she had come.

Despite the attempt at avoidance some few minutes later she found herself crossing his path after all.

"Good evening, Miss Kingsland," he said in the bland, pleasant manner she did not trust in the least. "Do you enjoy the evening's entertainment?"

"So far, my lord, I am bound to own that it has been excellent."

"I am delighted to hear you say so. I'm persuaded, however, it can only improve." When she looked skeptical, he said quickly, his eyes lingering on the diadem, "The Truscott jewels become you very well, indeed, Miss Kingsland."

Sophia was certain she detected a note of disapproval in his manner so she contrived to answer in an even voice, "Thank you, my lord. The diadem is Lady Truscott's gift to me on the occasion of my betrothal. It is far too generous a gift, of course, but I would not for anything wish to offend her."

He smiled faintly. "It would be foolish for anyone to attempt to gainsay my aunt, and it is evident it is the first of many such gifts. There could be no more worthy recipient. It is to your credit you have wasted no time in displaying your gratitude so publicly."

His comments appeared to be perfectly sincere, but Sophia did not in the least trust his smooth tone, for she was fully aware he was a practiced tongue-pad. It seemed inconceivable to Sophia that he might just possibly believe she was marrying Felix for his aunt's jewels, fine as they were. Even if Lady Truscott had offered to give her all those she possessed, they were as nothing compared to the treasures nestling somewhere in the Manville family vault.

It was some relief to her when Felix came upon them at last. "Manville," he greeted his cousin. "Good to see you! Sophia, dearest, I have been seeking you out for an age."

Sophia cast a sweet smile at the earl. "Felix has been in much demand owing to his having met, albeit briefly, Senorita Malliende."

The young man rubbed his hands together gleefully while his cousin eyed him indulgently. "I'm in a deuced fidge to see Senorita Malliende dance, Manville." Then he amended. "Dash it all! Everyone to a man is in a fidge to see her."

"You will not be obliged to wait for much longer," the earl answered and he looked, for once, uncertain. "I do hope no one will be disappointed."

Felix laughed at the very idea. "I have never seen such anticipation in any audience."

"I recall even more excitement when there was the prospect of seeing a dancing horse at Astley's," Sophia pointed out, looking guileless, and the two gentlemen cast her frowning glances.

"By the by," the earl said moments later, "Lady Truscott and Senorita Malliende are now ensconced in our aunt's house in Tavistock Square."

"That should confound the tattle-baskets," Felix answered in a hearty tone. "No one can impeach Aunt Truscott's honor."

The earl's smile was rather strained. "Just so."

He glanced briefly at Sophia, bowed and said, "By your leave," and walked back in the direction of Lady Whitchurch's box.

Both Felix and Sophia watched him go and then she said briskly, "It is time for us to return, too, Felix. We would not wish to miss one moment of the second half."

"No, indeed not," the young man agreed, oblivious to her heavy irony.

As they made their way back, he said, "I have it in mind, dearest, that you have taken my coz in dislike."

"I fear there is little in him to admire."

"You are a quiz, Sophia. There are few enough females who could form such an opinion in so short a time. Indeed, I confess I have never known it before."

"You once declared your affection for me stemmed from the fact you considered me out of the ordinary."

"Quite so," he agreed, looking uncomfortable at the reminder, "but I cannot conceive why you should dislike Manville, who, you must own, is all amiability nowadays."

"Do you truly think so, dearest? I find I dislike his manner. It is regrettable and mayhap a fault in *me*, but it is nevertheless undoubtedly so."

The young man had scant opportunity to argue the matter any further, for when they arrived at the box, the others were present and the second half of the evening about to begin.

The beau monde was notoriously fickle about who and what it favored, but it was clearly evident from her very first steps on the stage that Manuela Malliende had won the admiration of almost everyone present. Even Sophia, who was bound to admit she was prejudiced, although she did not know why, was entranced by every delightful step. Even the young bucks in the pit remained silent throughout, which was very uncommon, and the moment she had danced her last step, the audience erupted into joyous applause.

"How splendid that was!" Sophia heard Felix exclaim through all the noise.

"Oh yes, indeed!" Captain Murchison agreed.

"I have always maintained that my coz has an unerring eye for all that is splendid," Felix whispered a moment later into Sophia's less than receptive ear.

It was several minutes before the new sensation was allowed to leave the stage, whereupon the boxes began to empty slowly at last and the young men in the pit almost stampeded in their anxiety to rush backstage to congratulate the performer personally. Glancing across at the Whitchurchs' box, Sophia's eyes met those of Lord Manville and he looked, as might have been expected, very pleased with himself.

On leaving the theater the crowds were even thicker than on arrival, owing to everyone being held back in order to allow the royal party to leave first. As the Kingsland party resigned itself to a long wait before their carriages arrived, all around them the talk was of Manuela Malliende's magnificent debut.

"I am famished," Celia complained.

"So shall we all be by the time we arrive back and have our supper," Captain Murchison told her, "but in all truth, it is worth the delay to have witnessed Senorita Malliende's debut."

"I cannot agree with you on that score, sir," Sophia replied.

"I would be delighted to have the honor of transporting the ladies back to Manchester Square in my carriage."

They all looked round to see Lord Manville standing to one side of them. His presence caused Sophia to start, for she had no notion he was so close by.

"What makes you believe your carriage will be sooner than ours?" Sir Magnus inquired.

"Because it is already outside and ready to depart, sir."

Sophia glanced at Felix, who looked admiringly of his cousin, and then back to the earl. "I think not, my lord. It would . . ."

"Oh, don't be so tiresome," Celia scolded, and then she glanced at the earl in her most coquettish manner. "My feet ache abominably and I confess I am truly famished. It is splendid of you to suggest you take us home, my lord, and I for one accept with alacrity."

Before Sophia had any further opportunity to consult with Felix, she found herself being propelled through the crowds by her friend, with Lady Kingsland and Jessica close behind. Miraculously a way was made for them and before Sophia could protest further, she found herself seated in the earl's very comfortable closed carriage.

When the ladies were inside, he followed them and the lackey slammed shut the door. A moment later the carriage set off, ahead of most of those which would choke the streets nearby for some considerable time to come.

"We are most obliged to you, my lord," Lady Kingsland told him while her elder daughter continued to look mutinous as she stared out of the window into the blackness beyond.

"I am glad to be of service, ma'am," he replied, eyeing Sophia with amusement. "I could not in all conscience stand by while my carriage was outside and ready to leave."

"I only wonder that Lady Truscott did not wish to avail herself of it," Celia pointed out, eyeing him curiously.

The earl cast her an urbane smile that caused the color to rush to her cheeks. "Her ladyship has returned to Lord Whitchurch's house. A large party is to go there for supper."

"Do you not wish to go there, too?" Sophia asked, looking at him at last.

"I daresay I shall join them in due course. However, in the meantime I am delighted to be able to do you this service, for you appear to be quite exhausted."

"You are mistaken, my lord," she snapped.

"My sister is always acting the mooncalf," Jessica said teasingly. "She cannot abide being parted from Felix for a moment."

"I am no such thing," Sophia protested and then, glancing at the earl, "but I certainly would not wish to put Lord Manville to any trouble."

"It is no trouble, I assure you, and you may be certain my cousin will soon join you for supper."

Sophia was exasperated at such an inference which was patently untrue, and her angry gaze fell upon the earl who looked as handsome as ever in his evening clothes. Not for the first time did she wonder what went on behind that dark countenance of his.

"Lord Manville, I'm persuaded poor Senorita Malliende will be waiting in vain to be conveyed to her house while you do us this very great service," Sophia persisted.

"Tush!" Celia exclaimed. "She will be engaged for hours yet at the Opera House with those who wish to congratulate her."

"Miss Waddell is correct," the earl affirmed. "I shall have no end of time to deliver you ladies to Manchester Square and return to Covent Garden. In any event, Senorita Malliende now has her own carriage. It would be inappropriate for her not to."

"Her own carriage!" Jessica enthused, her eyes bright. "How I envy her!"

"You have many of the advantages she has not, Miss Kingsland," the earl politely pointed out.

"My younger daughter is yet a goosecap, my lord," Lady Kingsland explained, looking at the girl reprovingly.

"You need have no fears for your younger daughter," the earl assured her. "I have no doubt at all she will become as laudable as her sister in due course."

Both Jessica and Celia giggled while Sophia just became wide-eyed, and then her face took on a flinty look, for she did not trust him in the least.

To Sophia's profound relief, the carriage arrived outside the house at that moment. The earl climbed down the moment it came to a standstill and immediately helped the ladies disembark. Sophia was the last and she noted sourly that Celia allowed her hand to linger in his rather longer than was warranted. The earl simply responded to her with his most charming smile, which enraged Sophia anew. The ink on Celia's engagement announcement was scarcely dry and she still persisted in flirting with any gentleman who crossed her path.

A moment later he handed Sophia down with great solicitude. In contrast to her friend she withdrew her hand immediately, nodding to him abruptly as she did so.

"Will you join us for supper, or is it definite you are to go to the Whitchurchs'?" Lady Kingsland asked.

The earl glanced briefly at Sophia who affected not to notice and then smiling regretfully, he declined, much to her relief.

"No doubt I will collect my aunt in due course, but I believe it best for me to return to the Opera House immediately. Senorita Malliende is still a trifle strange in this country and I feel responsible for her."

"She appeared supremely at home to me when I saw her the other day," Sophia felt bound to point out.

He looked deep into her eyes, which was a most disquieting experience. "As with most people, Miss Kingsland, all is not always apparent by what one shows to the world at large." He bowed before climbing back into the carriage, saying, "Good evening, ladies."

As the carriage set off back to Covent Garden, the four ladies went into the brightly lit hall to be relieved of their mantles by the footmen on duty.

"It has been a most splendid evening," Lady Kingsland declared, and led the way to where a supper had been laid, "especially as we have contrived to arrive back with the minimum of delay."

"It would have been even better if Lord Manville had consented to join us for supper, Mama," Jessica added.

"There is something quite challenging about that man, don't you think?" Celia mused, looking from one lady to the other in turn.

"Tush!" Sophia answered, pushing her way angrily in front of them into the supper room even though food was the last thing she wanted.

For some reason she could not quite fathom the evening had not in the least turned out in a satisfactory manner.

Seven

Since he had returned to London, a hero of the war against Napoleon, the talk had been in polite circles quite naturally of little else except the Earl of Manville. Now, his protégée, Manuela Malliende, had replaced him as the main topic of conversation in the salons of the *ton*. Even Wellington's victories in the Peninsula were not remarked upon as often as Senorita Malliende's wonderful dancing.

Since her triumphant debut at Covent Garden Opera House, Manuela Malliende had played to a packed house every time she appeared. The management of the theater was known to be delighted with her success, Lord Manville was bound to be equally pleased, and the *ton* was in a lather of admiration for the Spanish dancer.

Felix Harcourt declared himself scarcely able to wait until he could see her dance again.

"In truth I did not find her so remarkable," Sophia told him in a cool manner after he had made the declaration countless times, silencing for a while his enthusiasm.

While Manuela's success irked her as much as Felix's admiration of her, Sophia could not blame him his feelings, for almost every buck was entranced by the waif-like Spanish girl. It had been said that if the same volume of flowers and gifts continued to arrive at her house in Tavistock Square, Senorita Malliende would be obliged to move to a larger establishment to accommodate them.

As Sophia browsed around Mr. Browne's circulating library a few days later, musing on the astounding success of Senorita Malliende, she wondered idly if Lord Manville would one day marry her, as so many were suggesting he might. It was by no means unheard of for someone of such high birth to marry an opera-dancer, but somehow she thought that the earl was far too conscious of his position in society to do so. However, she did acknowledge he was the type of gentleman who wouldn't give a fig for any social convention if he wished to pursue some course or other.

Still deep in thought as she fingered a copy of *Childe Harolde's Pilgrimage*, which in truth she had already read on several occasions, all at once she heard a familiar voice calling her name.

When she looked up, it was to see Celia Waddell bearing down upon her, exhibiting an ominous air of excitement. "What good fortune it is to find you here. I had resolved to call upon you in Manchester Square with no further delay."

Her eyes were bright, which suggested to Sophia that her friend was about to reveal a snippet of particularly lurid gossip.

"Whatever can have put you in this taking, Celia?" Sophia asked, not troubling to hide her amusement.

"I was never more surprised in my life! I was on my way to partake of tea with Lady Murchison yesterday and we were obliged to pass through Tavistock Square . . ."

"How pleasant that must have been for you, dear."

Miss Waddell clucked her tongue with annoyance. "You do know who lives in Tavistock Square, do you not, Sophia?"

"A great many people, by all accounts," her friend replied, feigning an air of indifference.

"Oh, you are so provoking of late, Sophia, I cannot conceive what ails you since you have lately made such a brilliant match. You should be in high snuff."

"How can you doubt that I am?"

Miss Waddell waved one gloved hand in the air. "Oh, it is of no consequence. What I wished to relate was *who* I saw coming out of Senorita Malliende's house!"

"If you intend to tell me it was Lord Manville you must own he is entitled to visit his protégée."

"I could not agree with you more, but it was not Lord Manville; it was Felix I saw."

Sophia's eyes grew wide with shock. "You must be mistaken."

"I vow to you I am not! How could I be mistaken? If I did not know Felix Harcourt almost as well as

95

I know you, there might be some room for doubt, but there was certainly no mistaking the color of his high-perch phaeton, which was parked outside! Moreover, Tom tells me that when Lord Manville took us home after Senorita Malliende's debut, they both went backstage to congratulate her!"

For a few moments Sophia was stunned into silence and then she rounded on her friend. "Really, Celia, you must be singularly lacking in interesting *on-dits* to relate to me such insignificant tarradiddle. Almost every buck in town must have called upon Senorita Malliende since her debut. There is nothing in the least remarkable about it."

Miss Waddell had little time to remain taken aback by her friends's waspishness before her mother called out to her and she was gone, looking unusually subdued. Sophia snatched up the book of poetry and called to her maid, who was at that moment engaged in conversation with several other abigails awaiting their mistresses.

When they walked outside into the bright sunshine, Sophia didn't know whether she was angry or sad. As she had told Miss Waddell in no uncertain terms, it was not in the least unusual for young gentlemen to call upon famous singers or dancers to show their admiration, but somehow she would not have expected it of Felix, of all people. In all truth she had never seen him so much impressed by anyone, even noted artistes who regularly performed at fashionable theaters.

"Miss Kingsland!"

Her head snapped up to see the earl coming across Bond Street in her direction. She had been so deep in thought she had not noticed that his curricle was parked at the opposite side.

"What a pleasant surprise," he told her and she bobbed a curtsy. "Will you by any chance be seeing Felix this afternoon?"

"It has not been arranged, but I daresay it is possible that I might," she told him, adding sourly, "Felix has formed a penchant for unexpected calls."

Quite evidently he had no notion of what she meant and continued, "If you do, I beg you to tell him the mill at Settringham has been postponed."

"That is, I fancy, no calamity, my lord. After all, as I recall he attended a mill on Tuesday, a horse race on Wednesday and made several visits to Tattersall's, but I am sure I have no need to tell *you*, for you accompanied him on every occasion."

He looked wry. "You must understand, after such a lengthy absence I do need to restock my cattle, Miss Kingsland, and I value Felix's opinion in such matters."

"Not as much as he values yours, I'll warrant."

Much as she hated herself for it, Sophia could not prevent the note of censure creeping into her voice, and he said pointedly, "I am glad to see you have decided to patronize Browne's library here in Bond Street and not the one in the Strand."

Ignoring the pink flush that invaded her cheeks at the reminder, he noted the book in her hand. "Byron has become something of a celebrity in my absence. Who would have thought it?"

"His poetry is quite remarkable," she felt bound to say.

"So I am given to understand. I am lost for admiration, if only because his genius allows for his

97

outrageous behavior, but what hope is there for the rest of us?"

Sophia could not help but smile. "I cannot imagine *you* penning romantic poems."

"Nor can I, in all truth," he answered with a laugh, "but what is a reformed rake to do?"

All at once Sophia was assailed with a wish that they had not encountered each other for the first time in those unfortunate circumstances. It might have been possible for her not to dislike him quite so much if she had first met him at her mother's rout in Manchester Square.

"Reformed, my lord?" she asked, looking amused for once.

"Of course, we do have a little in common, Byron and I," he went on, ignoring her question. "We both have the ability to outrage and we are fond of visiting Jackson's gymnasium."

Sophia glanced across the road to where many bucks of the *ton* were coming and going to the famous establishment to be instructed in the art of fisticuffs by the now retired fighter.

"I did not think for one moment you were shopping in the mercer's and linen-draper's," she responded.

"There seems to be a rumor that although I appear to be hale and hearty, in truth I am unable to do anything remotely onerous without reducing myself to a wreck. It seemed opportune to show what I am still capable of doing at the gymnasium."

Belatedly Sophia recalled suggesting to Celia Waddell that he was able to partake of only one dance in an evening due to the severity of his injuries, and she suspected that was the source of this particular *on-dit*.

"Those who know you could not doubt your prowess," she assured him, feeling a trifle guilty.

"You flatter me unduly, ma'am, but no doubt now that it has been seen to be so no one will doubt my return to full health." He smiled wryly again. "Unfortunately only gentlemen were present at Jackson's, so the tale will be a little slow in being circulated, which is a great pity, you must own."

"Shame on you, Lord Manville!" she teased, beginning to enjoy the conversation with him. "Do you truly believe it is only females who exchange *on-dits*?"

"Oh no, Miss Kingsland, some of them invent them." His smile faded and he stepped back a pace. "No doubt you are anxious to be gone from here so you are able to read your poetry."

"I don't really know why I chose it, for I have read it often before. Perchance you would like to borrow it in my stead?"

"No, I thank you. I don't believe I should add the reading of poetry to the long list of vices of which I am believed guilty," he replied, holding up his hand in mock horror.

"If you mean me to understand you care about what people say of you, my lord, then I must accuse you of gammoning me."

"Only in the gentlest way, Miss Kingsland," he admitted.

For once there was little abrasiveness between them, and all at once Sophia was thrown into confusion. She was forced to look away from his searching gaze and to hide her discomfort, she began to move closer to the carriage where Lily was already ensconced.

"I really must return home, my lord ..." she murmured.

He brushed aside the lackey and opened the door of the carriage for her himself, handing her inside with great punctiliousness.

"If you are to attend Almack's this Wednesday evening, mayhap you will be good enough to reserve for me the quadrille, Miss Kingsland."

Sophia sank into the squabs before looking out of the window at him in some surprise. "Almack's, my lord?"

"You do have vouchers?"

Her lips curved into a smile. "Yes, indeed, I do, but I would scarce credit you with a wish to attend so dull an establishment."

"Dull? Do you truly regard it as dull, Miss Kingsland? I have it in mind that young ladies spend much of their time angling after vouchers for Almack's, and when they are obtained, cry roast meat to all those less fortunate."

Sophia could not help but laugh at the truth of what he said. "That is undoubtedly so, but it is equally true that many gentlemen who regard themselves as pinks of the *ton* dislike the place hugely for its lack of interest. It is a great paradox you must own."

"Mayhap my enjoyment is not always as others perceive it, ma'am. Good day to you ..."

As the carriage set off, Sophia observed him through the window as he recrossed the road. She craned her neck further when she caught sight of him greeting Lady Whitchurch. A moment later he handed her up into his curricle and Sophia sat back again, her expression becoming stony.

"Not as others perceive it, indeed!"

Lily sat forward then. "I beg your pardon, ma'am?"

"It is nothing, Lily." She glanced down at the slim volume of poetry cradled in her gloved hands. "Lord Manville and Lord Byron have a deal in common, I should say."

"Miss Kingsland, I have just realized who his lordship reminds me of!" the maidservant cried and her mistress looked at her in alarm. "That cove in Leeke Lane. Yes, indeed he does!"

"I really cannot conceive why it signifies if I called in on Senorita Malliende," Felix protested as he and Sophia sat at the edge of the dance floor at Almack's. "I was, after all, only one of scores who called in with flowers in the wake of her debut. As she is my cousin's protégée I could scarce ignore her remarkable achievement."

"What signifies is that I resent hearing of it from Celia Waddell!" Sophia explained, her manner stiff and proper in the extreme.

"I do beg your pardon on that score, Sophia. That chit is the most tiresome female I know. How was I to know she was calling upon Murchison's mama at that precise time? I have had no opportunity of telling you before she rushed to you with the news, if indeed it can be deemed such a thing."

As Sophia acknowledged to herself the truth of his words, he added, "You would do well to call upon her yourself."

"Indeed, I will not," she protested. "How dare

you suggest it? Even your cousin would not have the temerity to make such a suggestion."

"Sophia, let me assure you that Senorita Malliende is no lightskirt. My aunt's presence assures her respectability."

"All it signifies is that Lord Manville is exceedingly clever in his use of people close to him, but if you wish to make a cake of yourself by toadying to that creature, so be it! Let it not be said I am overbearing in this matter."

Mr. Harcourt looked outraged. "Overbearing, no. Impossible more like. The truth is, Sophia, you are swiftly becoming a scold. I cannot prevent you taking both Manville and Senorita Malliende in dislike, but do not, I beg of you, expect it of me."

All at once Sophia was chastened, able to understand Felix's annoyance, for the matter scarcely warranted such harsh words from her.

"Felix, I do beg your pardon most heartily. It was only hearing of it from Celia that put me in such a pucker. You cannot conceive of how it angered me."

"You have made it exceedingly evident, my dear," he answered stiffly. "I just wish everyone would not insist upon assuming that Senorita Malliende is my cousin's lightskirt, 'cause it ain't true. She comes from a well-connected family in Spain. She is, in fact, related to the Marques de Villanova."

Sophia's disparaging laugh carried easily around the room. "Oh, Felix, dearest, how could you believe such a Banbury Tale?"

When she laughed again, the young man frowned darkly. "Sophia, you are being very provoking this evening."

"Again I must beg your pardon, dearest, but that sounds like such tarradiddle. If I did not know you the better, it would almost appear you are acting the mooncalf."

His cheeks took on a ruddy hue. "That is a nonsense and you know it."

Just at that moment Sophia noticed that Lord Manville had arrived, dressed as always with immaculate care and extreme elegance. He paused in the doorway to glance around the room. Sophia wasn't certain if he had seen her and Felix, but she doubted if his casual glance missed anything. Moments later Lady Whitchurch approached him and it was evident she intended to employ her every wile to entrance him anew, if she had not already succeeded in doing so.

Sophia watched him with interest as he conversed pleasantly with the lady who should have been his wife. They would have made a handsome pair, she thought.

"My admiration of Senorita Malliende is purely for her art," Felix was saying with studied care. "Even if you believe her to be a doxy, you are bound to own her talent which is prodigious."

Sophia returned her attention to him at last, regretting ever broaching the subject with him. "Her relationship with any member of society is of no account to me, I assure you. My concern is more for your relationship with Lord Manville. I know how you admire him and I would not for anything wish you to do anything which might antagonize him."

Felix looked startled. "I cannot conceive how I might do that."

With the utmost patience she explained. "If your

cousin harbors proprietorial feelings toward Senorita Malliende, he is not like to wish you to call upon her."

"Sophia, it was only the once, my dear." When the music struck up, he said quickly, "The quadrille. You always enjoy this dance so let us stand up for it."

"It is already bespoken," someone answered before she had any opportunity to reply.

The young couple looked around in surprise to find the earl standing nearby. Felix jumped to his feet, his face breaking into a smile of genuine pleasure.

"With you, Manville? I had no notion. Sophia did not make mention of it to me."

"You do not mind?"

"Lord Manville," Sophia began to protest, but Felix went on to say in a hearty manner, "I most certainly do not. Sophia and I will have many opportunities to stand up together later in the evening."

Smilingly the earl held out his hand to her and she went to him, surprised at her own docility. There had certainly not been any opportunity for him to bespeak any of the dances that evening and she did wonder why Felix had not realized it.

As they took their places in the set, they were watched by her husband-to-be and many other curious people. It was certainly a more enjoyable dance than on the previous occasion. The earl's injuries had not curtailed his ability on the dance floor and he was able to prove that quite clearly to one and all.

"How pleasant to see you making an effort to be

amiable toward your cousin's future wife, Manville," Lady Whitchurch commented as the earl escorted Sophia back to the edge of the floor when the dance was ended. "Moreover, it is evident Mr. Harcourt intends to curry favor with you by calling upon Senorita Malliende. It is exceedingly equitable."

"What on earth did she mean by that remark?" the earl inquired when the marchioness had passed by on the arm of Lord Pinkton.

Taking a deep breath, Sophia explained that Felix had called upon Senorita Malliende after which the earl remarked, "I know Felix could only be one of many, so I wonder why she troubled to mention it to me. It is nothing out of the ordinary."

"We have, I fear, Miss Waddell to thank for any tattle, my lord. She observed him leaving the house and found the occasion remarkable enough to mention to me."

He cast her a curious glance. "I am glad to note the *on-dit* has not put you out of countenance, Miss Kingsland."

Sophia laughed and fluttered her fan. "La! Why should it do so? Felix is at liberty to do exactly as he pleases and no one doubts that Senorita Malliende is deserving of any praise a gentleman is like to heap upon her."

"That is exceedingly generous of you, ma'am."

She was about to take her leave of him when the music struck up again and this time it was a waltz that was announced. The earl drew her back toward the dance floor, although she made some small protest, glancing around her in alarm as the gossips began to chatter behind their fans.

"We are not engaged to stand up for this dance," she protested.

"Take pity upon me, Miss Kingsland. I must stand up again so that all can see I am no cripple."

"Oh fie! I am persuaded everyone already has no doubt that you are now entirely recovered from your injuries."

Nevertheless he whirled her into the stream of dancers and as he did so, she caught sight of Felix watching them and looking somewhat bemused. Despite her initial misgivings at dancing the waltz, and in particular with the earl, Sophia found that after a while she began to enjoy this relatively new dance, held close in the arms of a man she regarded as her enemy.

Once again she reflected on the unfortunate circumstances of their meeting. If only they could have met for the first time at her own rout, she would have felt more kindly toward him, she was sure.

When the waltz ended, Sophia's cheeks were flushed, but her eyes were bright. A little breathlessly she glanced around for sight of Felix, but he was now not to be seen.

The earl also noted his cousin's absence and said, "You look in dire need of some refreshment, Miss Kingsland. Allow me to escort you to the supper room where I shall procure a drink for you."

For a moment Sophia was tempted to refuse his invitation, but then, cooling her cheeks with her fan, she nodded her assent. Many pairs of eyes noted their departure from the ballroom with great interest.

It was mercifully more cool and quiet in the adjoining room, although the noise of music and laughter could still be plainly heard, but not to the exclusion of conversation. Wearily she sat down while the earl brought her some lemonade. Just then Lady Whitchurch and Lord Pinkton entered the supper room and Sophia couldn't help but wonder if the timing was as coincidental as it appeared.

Lady Whitchurch was, as always, exquisitely attired in the latest fashion and her person was liberally adorned with many of the Whitchurch jewels. The couple paused as they came abreast of the earl and Sophia, smiling and nodding affably.

"How odd it is to see you here, Manville," the marchioness ventured. "You was never used to be fond of Almack's. Indeed," she added with a laugh, "if you persist in presenting such a conventional face to us all, it is like to be said you are dangling after a wife."

The earl regarded her from beneath his long, dark lashes, which were lowered so far there was no telling the look in his eyes. "Far more outrageous things have been said of me, my lady."

She sketched an ironic curtsy and they moved on. Sophia watched her for a moment or two and then returned her attention to the earl. "It must be difficult to live up to or live down a notorious past, my lord."

"You have evidently observed the difficulty." He drew up a chair which seemed too frail to support his large frame and sat down beside her. "Have you decided which of it I am doing?"

"I . . ." Sophia fanned her cheeks once again. "I am persuaded, my lord, it is no concern of mine."

After a moment's pause he went on, "I have hoped for a quiet moment with you for some time."

107

Her eyes widened in alarm as he went on, "It occurred to me quite recently, and for that I must beg your pardon, that I had not properly apologized for my atrocious behavior the first time we met."

She started and began to assure him hastily, "Oh, I am persuaded you have already done so, my lord."

"Well, I do hope you take it I am thoroughly ashamed of myself. I would not for anything wish to cause distress to any young lady. What occurred was the result of a momentary urge and, naturally, I did not expect us ever to meet again, not that that is sufficient excuse, for I am fully aware that it is not."

Although she could detect no trace of insincerity in either his expression or his manner, Sophia laughed harshly. "Lord Manville, I cannot for anything, understand your concern for my feelings after so long a time has passed."

He raised the glass of lemonade, which looked so incongruous in his hand. "Is it not evident why I am so concerned?"

Her heart began to beat very strongly then and she averted her eyes from his. "It is not in the least evident to me."

"I would not wish you to set your face against me. You will before long marry my cousin and I would not wish for anything to be at daggers drawn with you. I have too much regard for Felix to wish for anything other than a perfect accord with his wife."

Sophia drew a deep sigh, although she did not truly know why his declaration depressed her so. "You will always be welcome in our home, my lord," she answered, feeling not in the least heartened. "The matter to which you refer has long since been banished from my mind."

"Ah, so there you are!" Felix greeted them the moment he came into the room. "A Scottish Reel is about to begin, and this time it is *my* turn to stand up with you!"

Eight

Sophia walked briskly along the corridor past an extensive display of family portraits toward her mother's dressing room, glad that yet another session with her mantua-maker was at an end.

As she approached the room, Jessica came out and cast a sharp look in her sister's direction. "Why do you look so Friday-faced, Sophia? You would not think to look at you, you were about to be married to a most eligible bachelor *and* possess vouchers for Almack's. In your shoes *I* should be as gay as a goose in a gutter."

A fleeting smile passed her sister's lips. "You would not if you had been obliged to stand for hours being pinned, pushed, and prodded by the mantua-maker. She will tolerate nothing less than perfection in her work."

"With so much rivalry abroad you ought to be heartily glad of that."

Her sister sighed. "In truth, Jess, I had not thought so many gowns necessary for just the one Season."

"It is not just the one! Next Season you will have an establishment of your own, and no doubt need even more gowns to conduct your social life as the Honourable Mrs. Felix Harcourt!"

"La! It isn't possible to be more hectic than we are now," Sophia answered with a laugh.

"Only think, you will be holding your own balls and routs at Grosvenor Square. Moreover, if Lord Rexton goes to Peg Trantum, you will become Lady Rexton, and it will be desirable for you to chaperon me."

"Perish the thought!"

"Unless, of course, you are increasing next Season."

"What humbug you speak, Jessica," her sister replied in outraged tones.

"You must own that it is entirely possible."

"Is Mama at home?" Sophia asked pointedly. "I wish to have words with her."

"She is indeed at home, but she does have Lady Abbotsbury with her and as you might surmise the *on-dits* are endless. It will be devilishly difficult for you to have words with Mama now."

Sophia nodded, looking rueful. "I can well imagine. I suppose I should not ask if there was anything of interest in the gossip."

"It is very much of the usual. Prinny had an apoplectic fit at Carlton House last night and was relieved of twenty-six ounces of blood. I believe it was this snippet of news that brought her ladyship round here."

"You really should not call His Royal Highness, Prinny, Jess. It isn't respectful."

"All his cronies call him that."

"That may well be, but you are not one of his cronies."

"There was an *on-dit* about Felix," Jessica said slyly.

"Felix?" Sophia echoed in alarm. "Pray, what can Lady Abbotsbury have to say about Felix?"

"It seems he has been seen in Tavistock Square outside number ten, and you danced the waltz and quadrille with Lord Manville at Almack's."

Sophia laughed again then, although there was a harsh edge to the sound. "How remarkable that sounds. No doubt her ladyship has made it all appear like a *ménage à quatre*, which is a nonsense. Since when can mere politeness be construed as anything else?"

"In the ranks of the *ton*, it can," Jessica answered.

"If we all contrived to cut each other, imagine the tattle that would ensue from that."

Suddenly Sophia caught sight of Felix entering the hall as she glanced over the balustrade. She gasped in surprise, but with no further ado she hurried down to greet him.

"Felix! I did not look to see you here today. What a pleasant surprise. I'm so glad you called in."

He beamed at her genuine pleasure in seeing him. "We seem to have parted brass rags so often of late, Sophia, I deemed it prudent to call in the event you would consent to go riding with me this afternoon. It would please me if you would."

Sophia smiled happily. "I would like that very

much. I will fetch my bonnet and pelisse immediately."

Only a few minutes later she returned, tying the strings of her bonnet. "You can do in minutes what other ladies take hours to achieve," he told her admiringly as he handed her onto the box of his phaeton, a carriage much envied by his peers.

He drove surely and skillfully, handling the team as well as any member of the Four-in-Hand Club. Sophia surmised that Lord Manville had taught him the rudiments of horsemanship when Felix was a boy, and she knew he could not have had a better teacher.

"It's horrid when we are out of countenance with each other, Sophia," he told her. "This is more like we was used to be."

"I take the blame entirely, Felix." He glanced at her in surprise as she went on, speaking in a resolute manner. "I know I have been greatly ill-humored of late, although I cannot conceive why it should be so."

"I have more than a suspicion as to why you have suffered the megrims of late. I have it in mind it has been only since your dreadful experience in Leeke Lane."

It was Sophia's turn to look startled. "Oh, do you really think so?"

"I am certain of it, and I am bound to say it is no wonder."

Toying idly with her gloves, Sophia bit her lip. "It was a great shock to my sensibilities, I must own."

"You need time to recover from the shock, that is all." He paused for a moment before glancing at

113

her briefly and then going on, "Crabtree told me the oddest thing which I am persuaded may account for a great deal of your ill-humor of late."

Her eyes narrowed somewhat as she cast him a frowning glance. "Crabtree? I don't recall hearing you speak of such a person before."

"He is my head groom. He was speaking to Baines while I was dining at your house the other evening."

"Oh?" Sophia regarded him curiously.

"According to your father's coachman, your abigail sees a strong resemblance in my cousin to the fellow who rescued you in Leeke Lane."

Sophia quickly stifled her anger toward her abigail and answered, "What humbug! They are not in the least alike. The chit must have windmills in her head to think so."

"Mayhap, but it is intriguing to suppose that you might harbor resentment toward Manville simply because he reminds you of what you wish to forget."

Such cleverness was not at all characteristic of Felix and, on this occasion, not in the least welcomed by his bride-to-be.

"It was my maid who saw a resemblance, not me," she pointed out, feeling uncomfortable. "And I do not harbor any resentment toward your cousin, I assure you."

He turned to grin at her. "I hoped that was so when I saw you dancing together at Almack's more than the once. It does my heart good to see you enjoying his company. There are few females, in all conscience, who would not."

They had reached the gates of Hyde Park and he

was obliged to slow down as they entered, joining countless others who rode or strolled at the fashionable hour, eager to see others and be seen by them. It was a great relief to Sophia that they were accosted on all sides by those eager to exchange a word.

As they made a slow progress, she could see Celia Waddell tooling the ribbons of an elegant whisky with Sir Frederick Carlyon at her side.

"Only recently betrothed and she still contrives to flirt," Sophia commented as the whisky passed by, the occupants waving to each other.

Sophia had still not forgiven Celia for gossiping so freely about Felix's call upon Senorita Malliende, but acknowledged, as there was no subterfuge in her future husband's actions, the girl could not be entirely blamed.

"It is the very first time I have heard you censure Miss Waddell," Felix commented. "You are always so loyal toward her, whatever she does or says."

"She is as always a dear friend, but I feel her flirtatiousness should now be curbed. She has made her choice in Captain Murchison and that should satisfy."

"How I agree with you on that score, dearest."

When she saw Lady Whitchurch approaching in her barouche, Sophia could not stifle a feeling of dismay. It was beginning to be familiar to see her with one admirer or another and the beau monde, Sophia knew, were waiting anxiously to see if Lord Manville was going to be claimed as her latest conquest.

Some considered it to be fitting that they should renew their old bonds of affection. Although they appeared handsome together Sophia thought that despite Lady Whitchurch's dazzling looks, the earl would soon tire of the company of such a chucklehead. In Sophia's opinion she had done him a kindness in crying off. However, she doubted if Lord Manville would consider it to be so. Suffering such appalling injuries so far from home, her disloyalty must have been a grievous blow.

"Good afternoon to you," the marchioness cooed, slowing her carriage as it came abreast of theirs. "It does my heart good to see you enjoying such felicity."

"We are obliged to hear you say so, ma'am," Felix answered, inclining his head in her direction.

"After the other evening at Almack's I would half expect to have seen you, Miss Kingsland, riding with Lord Manville, but," she smiled sweetly in Felix's direction, "I am persuaded there is a limit to what even cousins are willing to share."

As she drove on, Felix said, looking perplexed, "What the devil did she mean?"

"I rather think she considered herself a wit," Sophia answered with a sigh, "but in reality she is naught but a goosecap. Her excess of beauty is matched only by her lack of intellect."

The young man laughed. "Sophia, my dear, you have the makings of a great wit yourself. You can put a person down with one single word if you so wish."

Her eyes sparkled with amusement. "I do believe she is as mad as a weaver because I danced with Lord Manville the other evening and she did not."

"You are no doubt correct and I'll warrant she is as cross as two sticks she did not after all wait for

Manville to return from the war. She and Whitchurch are not as well suited in my opinion."

"The point is, she didn't expect him to return. We all know he was given notice to quit."

"She turned to Whitchurch in all swiftness, I assure you."

"One cannot truly blame her, Felix, but if she still harbors a fondness for Lord Manville, then we should pity her. It was a dreadful mistake to make."

"I pity any female who harbors a fondness for m'cousin. There must be a score—no, more!—females who still wear the willow for him, the scoundrel." He chuckled. "I was always prodigiously astounded at the number of females who were willing to make a cake of themselves over him."

"Did he make a habit of playing old Harry with females' emotions, Felix?" she asked, looking at him curiously.

"It was certainly one of his diversions, but although I deem the worst excesses well into the past, if I were a female, I would not risk throwing my cap over the windmill for Manville even now."

"Mayhap," she mused, "he is not quite so foolish. He is older and has undergone a profoundly frightening experience. I suppose it is possible he is now giving a thought to providing an heir to the title."

"I'll wager he has never given the matter a second's thought," Felix replied exhibiting astonishment.

Sophia smiled. "I'll warrant he did when he thought he had been given notice to quit and was leaving no heir to inherit the title."

The young man's eyes narrowed. "You seem to know a good deal of my cousin's thoughts, Sophia."

" 'Tis only supposition."

"The truth is, dearest, even I, who considers himself closest to Manville, was never able to gauge exactly what his thoughts were."

"You are not in the least like him in that respect," she told him with a laugh.

Their passage along the carriage paths was a slow one owing to the density of traffic and the many pedestrians in their way. Because everyone stopped frequently to exchange pleasantries or divulge the latest *on-dit*, it was a slow business riding in the park. Sophia had always enjoyed such excursions in the past, looking forward to hearing all the latest gossip in the process, but she had come to realize it was not always a pleasant matter being the subject of an *on-dit*.

Again, they were obliged to pause when hailed by yet another acquaintance. "Have you received your invitation to the prince's ball?" Captain Furness inquired from the saddle of his coal black mare.

"Not as yet," Sophia replied, "and it is always possible we may not do so."

"Sir Magnus is closely acquainted with His Royal Highness, ma'am, so I believe it is unlikely that your family will be excluded. Indeed, from all I have heard, *no one* will be excluded."

"Except Brummell and Alvanley," Felix suggested, causing the man to be convulsed with laughter.

"Speaking of Brummell, Harcourt, did you know he gave his arm to Manville for the entire length of St James's Street this morning?"

Felix's eyes opened wide with surprise. "No, I did

not. How famous! My coz is honored indeed. Dash it all! I would have liked to have witnessed that event for myself."

When they rode on a few minutes later, Sophia asked wryly. "Does this mean, perchance, that his lordship is going to consider himself even more top-lofty than he already does?"

"I should not be at all surprised," the young man answered good-naturedly. "Prinny may now be Regent, but it is certain Brummell still rules supreme in St. James's Street."

As they continued on their way, they were stopped on several occasions by those anxious to convey the story of Brummell and Lord Manville. After that it came as no surprise when the earl himself could be seen driving his curricle toward them. Sophia felt her breath dying in her throat when she caught sight of Manuela Malliende at his side, something that was bound to give rise to much more speculation about the pair.

Their progression through the park was even slower than most, for everyone wished to address the latest darling of the beau monde. Her red-and-white hat was quite magnificent, matching a fur-trimmed pelisse, all of which heightened the translucent whiteness of her skin and the glossy blackness of her hair.

"Did you know they were to be here?" Sophia demanded, glancing sharply at her husband-to-be.

"Of course I did not. How could I? I am not privy to my cousin's every move, but it is not so surprising, is it? Everyone else appears to be here today."

When the curricle drew abreast of the phaeton, the gentlemen raised their hats in the direction of the ladies, who nodded to each other, retaining a great degree of reserve as they did so.

"No one can gainsay me, Felix, when I declare we are escorting the two loveliest ladies in the land," the earl remarked.

"I shall certainly not gainsay you on that score," Felix assured him, gazing with blatant admiration upon the dancer.

Sophia's cheeks became tinged with pink, but Manuela Malliende said teasingly, "What tongue-pads you both are, gentlemen."

"I have not, as yet, had the opportunity to congratulate you on your stunning debut," Sophia told her.

"You are far too kind, Miss Kingsland. It is true we have seen little of each other since you called upon Lady Truscott, which is a great disappointment to me, I confess."

"While I naturally regret the omission, senorita, I confess that life at present seems to be so hectic. This is my first Season and it is particularly busy."

"How I envy you! However, you know you are always welcome at Tavistock Square whenever you are able to call. Moreover, I don't believe I am too bold in saying Lady Truscott would be glad to see you there also."

"Thank you, ma'am. Your invitation is kind and I will certainly bear it in mind."

"Heard all about your honor in St. James's Street this morning," Felix told the earl, drawing his rapt attention away from the Spanish girl at last.

"It is all the more surprising after I relieved him of a large purse last night at White's. However, unlike his prince, Brummell is never one to bear a grudge. Unfortunately we cannot dally here too long, for Senorita Malliende has to be at the theater tonight and is obliged to rest for a while beforehand."

Manuela Malliende dimpled and inclined her head as the curricle moved off. The dancer held her hat as she glanced back at the couple in the phaeton.

"I like your cousin very much indeed, Manville," she told him a moment later.

As Lord Manville skillfully maneuvered the curricle through the throng, he cast her a wry look. "I am fully persuaded, my dear, that my cousin likes you."

"Is it certain he is to marry Miss Kingsland?"

He glanced at her briefly once again. "As certain as such matters can be."

"What a pity that is," she mused. "I consider them unsuited."

"I am inclined to agree with you on that score, but Miss Kingsland and my cousin believe otherwise and there is little I can do about it."

"I was of the opinion you had a good deal of influence over him."

"In many areas I do, but in this I am bound to stand aside and leave him to his own devices."

"Nevertheless," she said thoughtfully, "I don't believe you will stand idly by and watch your cousin contract an unsuitable alliance, and if anything should occur to alter their plans . . ."

When he glanced at her again, there was a light of amusement in his eyes. "So that is the way of it. You are a scheming wench, Senorita Malliende."

Her eyes were wide and innocent. "Oh? What do

you mean, my lord? It is not me who schemes, I fancy."

She cast him a pointed look and his answer was only to laugh.

Traveling in the opposite direction, Sophia and Felix sat straight-backed in the box of the phaeton. Although they acknowledged the greetings of their acquaintances, they did not converse any further until he returned her to her home in Manchester Square, and then Sophia went into the house feeling in some manner that the day had not turned out as she would have wished.

Nine

The gaming tables at Brooks's Club were, as always, well patronized by the gentlemen of the *ton*. Through the years a great many fortunes had been won and lost there, and no one thought it amiss when entire estates were wagered on the turn of a card. In addition, many outrageous wagers appeared in the book, the latest being those for and against the possibility of the Earl of Manville marrying Senorita Malliende.

Well aware of the very public speculation about his life, the earl pocketed his modest winnings at whist and gave up his place at the table to another gentleman who was eager to participate in gaming, after which he began to wander through the various rooms in search of congenial companionship.

It took him some time to circumnavigate the rooms, for many of those who were not intent upon the serious business of gaming were anxious to claim acquaintanceship with him. In polite circles, where so much was public knowledge, he had returned to London that most curious of gentlemen— an enigma. He was certainly a gentleman to admire, excellent in all the pursuits beloved by those aspiring to be looked upon as Corinthians. Moreover, since his recovery from injuries considered serious enough to make an end of most men, he had been regarded by many as almost superhuman.

"I see that Manville has lost none of his skills at gaming," one gentleman remarked to another as they sat at a table in one corner of the room, enjoying a bottle of fine claret and gossiping about many of those who passed by.

In the gentlemen's club of St. James's, gossip was as enjoyable a pastime as that indulged in by their wives and mistresses in their drawing rooms.

"He was never used to be satisfied with so small a win—or loss," another answered, raising his quizzing glass to examine the earl more closely.

"Don't, on any account, underestimate that gentleman," remarked Lord Whitchurch, who was also observing the earl with great interest. "It is possible he has learned the art of discretion during his sojourn in the Peninsula."

"You may rely upon Manville, in the midst of war and chaos, to discover a beauty like the exquisite Manuela," Lord Smythe said in a sneering tone as he raised his glass to his lips.

"I have heard say she lives like a nun, with Lady Truscott in close attendance at all times. It is most unlike Manville to consort with such a creature."

"Just because she acts the nun with us does not necessarily mean she continues to do so when Man-

124

ville calls, unless his injuries were far more extensive than any of us can readily perceive."

The wit elicited a good deal of laughter from his
companions and while he was the focus of much
attention, the earl feigned nonchalance, even boredom, pausing frequently to speak to an acquaintance.

"Manville," Lord Steyning greeted him, "how do
you enjoy your return to London?"

"Very well indeed."

"I am bound to tell you you have proved to be a
great disappointment to your friends."

The earl's eyebrows rose a fraction. "It distresses
me to hear you say so, sir. Mayhap you'd be good
enough to explain why that is so."

The other man laughed. "Is it not obvious? You
have caused little tattle since you arrived back in
town. I have been obliged to wonder if this really
is my old friend who used to play old Harry all over
London."

The earl smiled. "Mayhap the fault lies more
with those who used to carouse with me all over
London. They have all, to a man, taken a wife"

Lord Steyning laughed again. "I cannot gainsay
you on that score, but I will have you know it is
not as painful an experience as you might suppose.
Perchance, you have it in mind, too, before long."

"Why should any female be foolish enough to
want to become leg-shackled to me?"

"You do yourself no credit at all, my friend. The
truth is you are still as eligible as ever you were.
You have retained your fine countenance and fortune, although one can scarcely credit why when
one recalls some of your youthful exploits, and I

daresay there are a score of females more than a little anxious to accept any offer you are like to make."

"Why is there this sudden interest in my bachelor state, Steyning? You are a good enough friend for me to ask it of you."

"You truly cannot wonder."

"Yes, I truly do," admitted the earl.

"Senorita Malliende."

"Ah!" the earl responded.

"Everyone is aware that she is refusing all advances made to her, so perchance she is already settled. At least that is what is being said."

"Senorita Malliende is anything but a goosecap so she would not tolerate me even if I were inclined to pay court to her. If she is much in demand, it is all to her credit, but she has great sense and will give herself time to choose wisely."

"There are many who will be disappointed to hear that, Manville."

"Are there so many eager to see me leg-shackled?"

"A great many would admire the lady who is able to bring that about. My wife, who I am bound to admit is quite a tattle-box, is in a fidge to know any morsel of information about you and Senorita Malliende. She has charged me to discover the veracity of the matter and it is more than I dare do to return home without a morsel of news."

"My apologies to Lady Steyning." The earl paused for a moment, a gleam of amusement coming into his eyes. "If you would but urge her and her cronies to be patient, mayhap they will be rewarded with news of quite startling proportions before too long."

The other man laughed uproariously. "If I tell her any such thing, I will have no peace whatsoever!"

"Oh, the trials of a tattle-basket."

"Or her spouse!"

The earl's smile faded somewhat when he glanced across the room beyond his friend. He quickly took leave of Lord Steyning and lost no time in going to where his cousin could be seen gambling liberally at vingt-et-un.

"Felix!" the earl said in an abrupt tone that caused the young man to whirl round in rather an unsteady manner.

"Patrick! I thought it possible to see you here, if not at White's."

The earl looked pointedly at the small pile of coins in front of his cousin. "What fortune have you had this evening?"

"You may hazard a guess from what you see." He sighed profoundly. "The truth is I am all dished up for this evening."

His cousin frowned. "It is quite unlike you to gamble to so deep."

"And unlike you to finish at this early hour."

"No one has ever credited me with sense enough to cry off at the correct moment, but it is time that they did."

"Why don't you put down your purse here? It will do my reputation no harm at all to game against a nonpareil like you."

"Not tonight, Felix," the earl answered in a tone

that brooked no contradiction, "and I believe it is time you called a halt for this evening."

The young man smiled. "You still regard me as a callow boy, Patrick. I'm not, you know."

"Then pray act the grown man. I see little of it just now. Recall, you will soon be a married man."

"Do not remind me," Felix answered laughingly. "Mayhap I do not have your good sense."

The earl's eyes narrowed slightly. "Do you mean to say you are regretting your decision to marry?"

Felix made a great effort to stand up straight without swaying too much. "Certainly not. I'll meet any man who dares to say such a thing!"

"Come along, Felix," his cousin urged briskly. "I am going to take you home."

The young man pocketed what was left of his purse and moved away from the table. His cousin at that point was obliged to lend a hand to steady him. "Just look around, Patrick. Are they not almost all married men who are gaming here tonight?"

When the earl made no answer, Felix asked, "What do you say we go back to my house and break open a bottle or two?"

"From all I have observed, Felix, I believe you have imbibed sufficient for this evening."

The young man shrugged away his hand. "Devil take it! You was never used to be such a prosy bore. Boney has a deal to answer for in what he did to you!"

"Come along now, Felix," the earl said firmly. "You are more foxed than you know."

Felix staggered into the lobby where his cousin gave quiet instructions to the lackeys.

"Those are fine words from the original five-bottle man," the young man replied.

A few minutes later Lord Manville had bundled his inebriated cousin into his carriage, having given instructions for Felix's phaeton to be driven home by the groom.

"Wanted to drive m'self," Felix mumbled as he almost fell onto the seat.

His cousin eyed him coldly from across the carriage. "If you aspire to become a five-bottle man yourself, Felix, you will be obliged to learn to take your liquor in a better manner than this. I doubt if Miss Kingsland would wish to see you in this condition."

Felix smiled faintly in the darkness. "You would like it if Sophia and I parted brass rags, wouldn't you, Patrick?"

"I cannot imagine why you should think so."

"You needn't seek to gammon me, coz. I know you too well."

"From what you have said tonight, I don't believe you know me at all," the earl responded in his most laconic manner.

Felix's lip curled at such a set-down. "Sophia was, after all, correct when she said you were against our betrothal and marriage. I can see that quite clearly now."

The earl leaned forward slightly and spoke in a soft tone. "If you wish me to be entirely frank, Felix, I believe Miss Kingsland to be far too good a catch for you."

The young man's eyes opened wide in surprise and then he leaned his head back against the squabs and began to laugh. "You are, as always, such a funster Manville."

The earl did not look in the least as if he were joking. In fact, he appeared to be rather grim-faced.

"Why are you not with Miss Kingsland this evening?" he asked, his tone becoming hard. "Since my return, I have observed you rarely far from her side."

"You should be able to hazard a guess as to the reason for that, Patrick. There is no place for gentlemen when weddings are being planned."

"So the arrangements are going forward a pace?"

"In those circumstances what is a fellow to do? I went to see Senorita Malliende instead."

"You must most truly be lost for love if an evening deprived of your future bride's company turns you into a suck bottle."

"No need to exaggerate, coz."

"Don't trouble to deny it, Felix. It is evident just by looking at you."

"Well, a gentleman needs no excuse to get a trifle bosky occasionally, and let me tell you there is nothing wrong with love. It is sublime."

The earl cast him a wry look. "I am truly delighted the evening has been so successful."

"None more so. Senorita Malliende makes any evening an experience of great pleasure."

"Senorita Malliende?"

"Yes, did I not say so? I went to Covent Garden to see her dance and then afterward a few of us called in to convey our admiration before we moved on to Brooks's. She was most, most gracious to us. For once you have done something to enrich us rather than scandalize."

The earl sat back, smiling slightly, both hands resting on his silver-topped cane. "I can assure you, Felix, I have lost none of my ability to scandalize. Incidentally, I must tell you that your regard for Senorita Malliende is not entirely one-sided. She confided in me her admiration of *you* when last we conversed together."

The young man smiled foolishly. "Really? I had no notion of that."

"Would I lie to you on such a matter? By the by, Senorita Malliende is now engaged to dance for His Royal Highness at his ball at Carlton House. Quite an honor, don't you think?"

"It will be the highlight of the evening without any doubt," Felix mumbled, and then he fell silent.

Watching him in the semi-darkness of the interior of the carriage, Lord Manville smiled to himself in a self-satisfied manner.

"I have been in a fidge to have words with you, Lily," Sophia said in such a severe tone it caused her maidservant to look somewhat alarmed.

With a steaming cup of chocolate in her hand, Lily closed the door of the bedchamber and came across the room. "I trust that you have found nothing amiss, ma'am."

"It certainly is! I am, I confess to you, as mad as a weaver," Sophia continued as the cup was placed on her bedside table.

"Oh, ma'am, I do trust that is not due to some omission of mine."

"It concerns no one else. You told Baines, who told Mr. Harcourt's groom, that Lord Manville reminded you of that . . ." she averted her eyes, ". . . gentleman in Leeke Lane."

"But he does, ma'am! I know he was no real gentry-cove, even though he did talk like the Quality, but he did look like his lordship to me and there's no getting away from it."

"So you have already taken great pains to tell me, but that is not precisely why I am angry. Do you recall vowing to me not to talk of the matter to the other servants?"

"I most certainly do, ma'am, and I have not spoken of it to a soul, I assure you."

Sophia clucked her tongue with impatience. "Lily, if you did not speak of it, how on earth could Baines tell Crabtree anything?"

The girl's face cleared. "Well, yes, I did tell him of the resemblance, but I had resolved not to tell that the gentleman had . . ." Lily bit her lip. "I mean, I never told anyone what he did, ma'am, and I wouldn't do so even under threat of torture."

"This sounds most intriguing."

Both Sophia and her abigail looked around to see that Jessica had come into the room and was quietly closing the door.

"It is none of your concern," Sophia told her. And then, looking at her maid, "You may go and prepare my toilette now, Lily. We will not speak of any aspect of this matter again."

The abigail looked more than a little relieved to be allowed to continue with her work with no further admonishment from her mistress. As Lily hurried into the dressing room to prepare the toilette, Jessica came across the room and sat down on the edge of Sophia's four-poster bed.

"All that talk of torture sounded intriguing to me."

"It was not in the least," her sister told her, taking up the cup. "Lily has learned to read, which in my opinion is not a trait to be encouraged in any servant. She has become addicted, I fear, to Mrs. Radcliffe's gothic tales. That is all."

The girl looked disappointed. "It sounded of much more interest than that to me. I thought all talk of 'he' had ended when Felix came up to scratch."

"It was not such talk as you imagine."

Jessica looked wry. "No doubt Lily has been acting the hoyden with Baines again and you feel unable to explain it to me. I do know of such things, Sophia."

"Well, you should not."

When her sister did not appear anxious to pursue the subject, the girl persisted, "I should have guessed it was not Felix who you were discussing. Well, one cannot expect him to do anything exceptional. That really would be outside of enough."

"Jessica!" Sophia looked shocked. "Are you criticizing Felix because he does not outrage?"

"No! He is the dearest man, but not in the least stimulating. You must own that is true."

"I own nothing of the kind. Moreover, I cannot conceive what you would wish him to be. I have always found him to be entirely congenial."

"Oh, I also own that he is, Sophia, but considering he and Lord Manville are such close kin, they are not in the least alike."

"Heaven be praised for that!" Sophia replied, directing her eyes heavenward. "If Felix was anything like his cousin, I would not be preparing to marry him."

"I cannot see where Lord Manville is such a scapegrace. Can you truly believe he was such a rakehell in his youth, Sophia?"

"Why should I not? His behavior was well observed by very many at the time."

"I was beginning to wonder if it were just a myth, for I have seen little sign of it so far. I confess it is quite a disappointment." While her sister cast her a rueful look, Jessica went on, "He has appeared to be quite conventional since he came to town. Why, there has only been the slightest hint of scandal attached to his relationship with Senorita Malliende."

"A hint would be more than sufficient for most gentlemen."

"If the tattle-baskets are to be believed, discretion was never one of his strong suits."

"Oh, I do wish you would not be so addicted to tattle, Jess. In any event just because Lord Manville has not gone around fighting duels every sennight, outraging gentlemen by flirting with their wives at every diversion, or losing items of the family jewels at the gaming tables, does not mean he has lost his propensity for mischief." Sophia was thoughtful for a moment before she added, "It is entirely possible he is still capable of causing a deal of trouble in much more subtle ways than he used to."

For a moment Jessica did not reply and then she said, "You really have taken him in dislike, haven't you?"

Without replying, Sophia threw back the coverlet

and swung her legs out of bed. "I cannot stay here any longer. Mr. Lawrence is coming here this morning to work on my portrait."

"You are always so busy nowadays," Jessica accused. "We never have time to enjoy a coze anymore."

"Tush! I thought we *were* just enjoying a coze."

The girl stayed where she was, sitting on the counterpane, smiling mischievously at her sister who, still clad in her night shift, went to peer out of the window into the garden.

"I can also hazard a guess as to why you have taken his lordship in so much dislike."

Sophia turned on her heel. "You talk a good deal of nonsense, my dear. In truth, I don't wish to listen to any more of it."

Jessica jumped to her feet. "You're such a Friday-faced creature nowadays, and all because his lordship monopolizes your dear Felix's time. That is what really miffs you about Lord Manville, isn't it?"

She didn't wait for her sister's answer as she hurried back toward the door while Sophia watched her wide-eyed.

As she opened the door, the girl paused. "I came in only to tell you we have received our invitation to Carlton House this morning."

"Oh, how wonderful!" Sophia declared, her manner brightening immediately.

"At least all of you have your invitations. As I have not yet been presented at court, I cannot attend. Not that I am truly concerned. It will be such a squeeze no one will be able to dance or even see an acquaintance."

"I doubt if anyone will cry off for those reasons," Sophia told her smilingly.

Jessica looked eager again. "What shall you wear? The peach sarsnet?"

"Oh, very likely. However, the mantua-maker is to deliver a new evening gown tomorrow and I may well choose to wear that in its stead. Everyone will make certain they look very grand."

"Shall you dampen your petticoats to make them cling to you?" the girl asked, her eyes wide with speculation.

"Certainly not!" Sophia snapped. "What would Mama say? Indeed, what would Felix say?"

"I daresay he will say you look absolutely splendid."

"Well, I shan't do it and there's an end to it." All at once Sophia looked troubled. "Everyone will be in such a to-do over this diversion. We shall be obliged to visit the *plumassier* with no delay. There is bound to be a huge demand for feathers prior to the ball. I shall press Mama to go immediately after Mr. Lawrence has gone!"

Ten

Oxford Street was always one of the busiest thoroughfares in the city, but the knot of carriages around Mr. Botibol's establishment later that morning confirmed Sophia's suspicion that the *plumassier* was going to be inundated by shoppers prior to the hurricane planned at Carlton House. As unpopular as the Regent had become in recent years, invitations to his functions were still very much prized.

"At His Highness's last rout," Lady Kingsland recalled, as she and Sophia climbed down from the carriage, "I declare sufficient food was left over to feed Wellington's entire army."

"From all I have heard and observed, the Prince is quite capable of eating it all himself," Sophia replied, much to her mother's amusement.

"Oh yes, I'm afraid that might well be so, my dear. Poor Prinny. I recall when he was so handsome and a fine figure of a man in his youth. Now he has grown so stout whenever he moves, his corsets creak and one is in the devil of a fix not to laugh out loud."

"I do hope, if I am presented to him, I will not laugh, for I declare it will be most tempting to do so."

"You would not shame yourself in such a way, my dear," her mother assured her. "As I am often at pains to say: my elder daughter always behaves with the greatest propriety. If only I could rely upon Jessica to be so decorous, I could look forward to her debut with more equanimity."

Once inside the shop both Lady Kingsland and her daughter were well occupied, not only choosing suitable ostrich feathers, but conversing with the many acquaintances going about a similar task.

As Lady Kingsland selected the feathers to put in her turban, Sophia caught sight of Celia Waddell climbing down from her carriage, and her heart sank. It was some minutes later, however, that she actually entered the emporium seeing Sophia immediately.

"How fine you look, Sophia!" she enthused. "Your hat is quite perfect. I am envious, I confess."

"Tush, Celia! You look in rude health, I am glad to say."

The girl grinned. " 'Tis a wonder, I own. Such a social hurry-scurry we are obliged to endure. I am persuaded I shall be hagridden by the time my wedding day arrives."

Sophia looked amused. "It really is no wonder. You lead such a hectic life with so many gentlemen in tow."

Miss Waddell waved one hand in the air in a dismissive gesture. "I am all done up trying to find one gentleman who does not constantly sing the praises of that Spanish dancer."

"Surely not Captain Murchison, too?"

The girl nodded. "They are all past praying for, and I should have thought as she is Lord Manville's lightskirt, they would exercise more restraint. If I were a gentleman, I should not wish to cross swords with *him*."

"Felix assures me they have no relationship beyond what is totally proper."

Celia Waddell's lips curved into a mirthless smile. "Felix Harcourt is foremost among her toadeaters, as you well know!"

"Celia! How dare you say such a thing? Felix admires Senorita Malliende, but I take exception at anyone saying there is more to the matter than that."

Celia Waddell smiled. "It was an unfortunate turn of phrase that I regret most heartily." Before Sophia had any opportunity to feel gratified, her friend continued. "I am quite envious of you, my dear, for if the matter teases you, you show no sign of it and you always look as fresh as a daisy however late you retire." She glanced around her at last, eager for sight of familiar faces, "No need to hazard a guess why Mr. Botibol has a smile on his face today. It is evident we all have our invitations to the ball at Carlton House."

"It will be quite exceptional, I am sure," Sophia responded in a cool tone.

"I have been told Mrs. Fitzherbert declined to attend once she learned she was not to sit at the Prince's table at supper."

"How complicated his life has become."

" 'Tis no wonder with two wives, both of them estranged! More to the point, Senorita Malliende has been asked to dance, although I declare not to be surprised at that. By all accounts His Royal Highness was most impressed by her. Who would not be?"

"It seems wherever we go nowadays, Senorita Malliende is to be the main topic of conversation. I congratulate you, Celia, on learning this snippet of information before anyone else. You are indeed the harbinger of news in town!"

Miss Waddell looked taken aback by her friend's very obvious sarcasm. "I only wonder you did not know already."

"I cannot conceive why you think I should," Sophia replied, affecting an attitude of indifference. "*On-dits* about Manuela Malliende are becoming a trifle commonplace."

The young lady looked annoyed. "I know of it only because Mr. Harcourt told me," she snapped.

"Felix?"

"None other," Celia answered, unable to hide her satisfaction at her friend's surprise. "I was quite persuaded, when I saw him outside this emporium a few moments ago, he must be waiting for you, but that is evidently not so. I must beg your pardon quite heartily for the assumption."

As soon as she was able, Sophia extricated herself from her friend's company and went out into the street to find Felix, who was standing a few feet away from Mr. Botibol's establishment where she had been unaware of his close proximity. However, with her own father's carriage prominently nearby, he could hardly have missed knowing where she must be.

"Felix," she called in hurt tones. When he turned to acknowledge her with a smile, she hurried up to him, saying accusingly, "I have been in Mr. Botibol's establishment for some time, so why did you not seek me out?"

The young man's cheeks grew red. "I have not, as yet, had the opportunity, dearest. I was simply passing by when Miss Waddell accosted me, and you know how she can prattle on so. It was devilishly difficult for me to extricate myself from her."

Not doubting the truth of that statement, Sophia nevertheless went on, maintaining her frosty manner, "She imparted to me the news that Senorita Malliende is dancing at Carlton House, and that it was you who had told her."

"As far as I am aware, it is not a secret." He smiled again in the face of her continued coldness. "I say, it should be a most diverting evening."

"I do not doubt it for one moment, but how did you come to know about it? I am persuaded no one else knows as yet."

"It was I who imparted the information, Miss Kingsland."

Sophia immediately turned on her heel to find the earl strolling toward them, swinging his ebony cane in a carefree manner that immediately annoyed her anew. He took her hand and raised it briefly to his lips, his eyes meeting hers before she felt obliged to look away.

"What a becoming outfit you are wearing, ma'am."

Color crept up her cheeks at the realization she had on the same pelisse and hat she had worn on their first encounter in Leeke Lane.

Ignoring her evident embarrassment, the earl then looked to his cousin. "Do you not agree with me on that score, Felix?"

The young man, whose thoughts appeared to be somewhat far away, replied, "Oh yes, yes indeed. Sophia is always in high feather."

Belatedly she realized that Felix had been standing by the earl's curricle and his escutcheon was plainly to be seen on the coachwork. All at once she was angry again, with whom on this occasion she was not quite certain. Once again she turned to Felix, her lips curved into the semblance of a smile. "You two are to be seen around together a good deal of late. You must take care lest you are paired too often. Prinny and Lady Hertford, Byron and Caro Lamb, Brummell and Alvanley."

"What tarradiddle," protested the young man who looked discomforted.

To Sophia's surprise, the earl laughed good-naturedly. "I always considered you to be a fine wit, Miss Kingsland. More than ever I believe my opinion justified."

She had no choice but to smile, too, to indicate a jest, hating herself for growing so angry. It was perplexing not to understand why she had taken so much exception to Felix being with his cousin, except that she considered the earl to be a bad influence on her future husband.

"You cannot imagine, Miss Kingsland, how much

I look forward to your becoming a part of my family," the earl told her a moment later.

He was looking directly into her eyes once more and she was forced to avert hers yet again, but not before she had seen the mockery in his look. Suddenly Sophia was afraid. She knew him only by repute and she could not begin to fathom the machinations of his mind. So many had called him a devil and no doubt it was with good reason. She was quite certain there was more than seemed apparent behind the bland facade of his face.

"Good morning to you, Miss Kingsland, gentlemen," a voice called, which was just then a welcome diversion for Sophia.

All three looked to the road where a whisky had drawn up alongside the earl's curricle with great skill by the one-armed Lord Smythe. As everyone was well aware, Lord Smythe had lost his arm fighting a duel with the earl, and Sophia caught her breath, looking from one gentleman to the other. However all was apparently congenial between the two, although Sophia was aware Lord Smythe was not someone who was likely to forgive easily.

"A fine conveyance you have there," Lord Manville told him, his manner unexpectedly friendly.

"You are welcome to tool the ribbons whenever it pleases you."

"I do thank you for the offer, my lord, and I may yet take you up on it."

Lord Smythe's lips curved into what Sophia thought was a cruel smile. "Oh, I am fully aware that you have little time for such trivialities now Senorita Malliende is in town."

In Sophia's opinion some of the warmth had faded from the earl's manner as he replied, "I cannot imagine why you should think so."

"Come, come, Manville, you are too modest. Who could possibly blame you for your interest? The lady is quite delightful, and I am full of envy of you."

Throughout the conversation Felix had been staring down at the ground beneath his feet. Sophia had somehow contrived to force a smile to her face, although why she felt so tense she could not understand.

"Now she is launched in her career, Senorita Malliende has little time to devote to me," the earl admitted, although he did not seem in the least regretful. "However, I hope I shall always remain dear to her. She has, I believe, sufficient bucks in earnest over her to enable her to ride with a different one every day of the year."

The other man laughed. "Keep your secrets, Manville. You were always as close as oak." Sophia was certain she was not wrong in detecting a nasty tone to the man's voice at this point. "Have you heard? Poor old Whitchurch is quite persuaded he is being cuckolded, but cannot perceive how."

The earl moved closer to the whisky and Sophia clutched onto her reticule in alarm as he said softly, but very clearly, "He must be an addlepate if he does not know he has been cuckolded since the day he was wed, but do have a care who you malign, Smythe. You surely recall that heedless words have cost you dear in the past."

It was said in a friendly manner, but neither Sophia nor Lord Smythe could mistake the meaning behind his words.

Lord Smythe's color heightened considerably. "You mistake my meaning, I assure you."

"I am most relieved," the earl replied unsmilingly.

"A few of us could not help but speculate the other evening about your . . . protégée."

"Speculation is always a hazardous endeavor," the earl informed him.

"Someone ventured the theory that while she acted the nun, mayhap she is more like to be of the Covent Garden order."

Sophia gasped as she looked for Lord Manville's response to what was a calculated insult, so it was quite unexpected when Felix's face twisted into a mask of fury and he dashed forward, crying, "You will not insult a lady in my hearing and be allowed to escape the consequences!"

"Good grief!" the dandy replied. "I declare the cub would blow off my other arm!"

The earl stepped forward quickly and drew Felix gently back. "If you ever again speak of any lady in that manner within my hearing, you will meet me once more, and you may be certain I shall be more accurate in my aim next time. Now, be on your way, Smythe."

It was all done so quietly that scarcely a passerby noted the altercation. No one who heard the earl speak could have doubted his resolve. Lord Smythe certainly did not and Sophia felt considerable relief when he drove on the moment the earl stopped speaking.

"Felix, what a goosecap you are," she scolded, putting one hand on his arm. "You should know

Lord Smythe is always spoiling for a fight with someone or other."

The young man looked at once shamefaced. "The devil take him, Sophia! I could not allow him to speak in such manner. He could have insulted you."

"Come, Felix, let us go," the earl urged. "We are already late." He raised his hat to Sophia as he climbed onto the box of the curricle, followed by his cousin.

"Where are you two going?" she asked to bridge what appeared to be an awkward moment.

Felix did not answer. He appeared to be still seething by the encounter, staring in front of him sightlessly. However, as he took up the ribbons, the earl glanced down at her. His own manner was perfectly at ease and for him it was as if the unpleasant interlude had never happened.

"We are going to call upon Senorita Malliende. When he learned I was engaged to call upon her, Felix expressed a wish to join me. Have no doubt, Miss Kingsland, by the time you and he meet again, he will have regained his humor."

Sophia opened her mouth to make some comment, but the earl raised his whip, which he dashed over the back of his team, and the curricle moved away at a spanking pace.

"Was that not Felix and Lord Manville?" Lady Kingsland asked as she came up behind her daughter.

"Yes, Mama," Sophia answered automatically.

"Oh, what a pity I have missed them, for I should have liked to have spoken to them."

As they climbed into their own carriage, Sophia's mind was in a whirl. The image of what she had seen was still so fresh in her mind. She could not possibly forget Felix's furious face as he lunged toward the baron, nor the fact that it was Lord Manville who had cooled the fraught situation. It was so uncharacteristic of both of them.

The earl was as ever an enigma to her, but the fact remained that Sophia had never seen her husband-to-be in such a taking before. It was almost as if he had become a different person to the one she had agreed to marry.

Eleven

"If only you hadn't been obliged to witness that
unpleasant scene," Felix said later that evening
when they attended an assembly given by Lord
Manville at his home in Park Lane.

With Lady Truscott as his hostess, invitations to
the affair had been keenly sought after by members
of the beau monde. The earl's wealth and position
would have been sufficient to give rise to excitement at the prospect of a diversion at Manville
House, but with his dangerous reputation still in-
tact, coupled with the fact that he was a most eligible bachelor, it ensured a keen interest in
attending.

It was, in fact, not only the first diversion held
by the earl since his return to London, but the first
since he came into the title, which was one more
fascinating aspect of the affair to the *ton*. It was
seen as a sign that his rakehell ways were finally

over and he meant to settle down to a more responsible existence.

Sophia, for one, was not certain of that, but she was much more troubled by what had occurred in Oxford Street that afternoon, although she contrived to affect a carefree attitude so that no one could guess her inner confusion.

"It is of no real consequence, Felix," she replied. "Everyone knows Lord Smythe is ill-humored and bears your cousin a grudge over the loss of his arm, and it was, after all, Lord Manville, he wished to provoke. In my opinion Lord Smythe received all he deserved by calling him a cheat. Anyone of any intellect is fully aware that Lord Manville would do no such thing."

Felix looked at her in amazement. "I cannot credit that you are championing his cause."

She looked away quickly, feeling even more confused. "Your cousin may be guilty of many calumnies, but I own cheating is not like to be one of them."

"I am so glad you are of that opinion, dearest, for I know you will also agree that I could not stand aside and allow Smythe to speak in such a manner in front of you."

The couple were seated together in an alcove and no one could think it amiss that two young lovers should wish to converse in private. Sophia was grateful for the opportunity, for there was a good deal of late in Felix's behavior that puzzled her. If she was to be honest with herself, she knew her own behavior had been less than rational.

"If it was me you wished to protect, I feel bound to assure you I was not nursed in cotton."

He laughed. "Indeed you were, and I admire you for it, my dear."

Sophia suspected he was laughing at her and found herself stiffening.

"In any event your reaction was a trifle extreme. It was not me, after all, who Lord Smythe insulted this morning."

A faint tinge came into the young man's cheeks. "He was most unflattering about another young lady, and I could not possibly stand by and allow him to slander one so fair."

"I would not wish anything untoward to be said about Senorita Malliende, but, Felix, you almost fought a duel with Lord Smythe."

"Do you doubt I would have trounced him?"

"No disrespect to you, dearest, but it is acknowledged that since he lost the duel with your cousin, Lord Smythe had ensured he has become a crack shot with the one hand he has left."

"Even so, I would have been happy to meet him had the matter progressed so far," Felix avowed, speaking with a note of resolve Sophia had not noted in him before.

"No doubt, but I shall be forever grateful to your cousin for averting such a catastrophe."

"It is a blessing Manville has at last found favor in your eyes, even if it is only in this one small matter."

Ignoring his sarcasm she went on, "You know full well no good can ever come of dueling for either of the participants. The loser is like to die and the winner is obliged to flee the country. It is no secret that is why Lord Manville was sent to the Peninsula. I do trust you will give me your word you will not be so foolhardy in the future."

The young man pulled at his waistcoat and looked uncomfortable. "Much as I wish to please you in this matter, Sophia, I regret I cannot categorically resolve not to do so. If anyone was to insult any lady of my acquaintance in the future, I must reserve the right to defend them in any manner at my disposal."

Sophia drew a sigh of resignation and supposed she might have expected such an answer. At one time she could have guaranteed his willingness to acquiesce to her wishes. Increasingly of late he was becoming a stranger to her and she struggled not to show her distress and bewilderment.

Looking back, they scarcely seemed to be the same couple who that summer gleefully anticipated the publication of their betrothal announcement in the *Gazette*.

He looked at her at last and it seemed he had been avoiding that all through their conversation. "I did look to you to understand, Sophia."

She smiled at last and patted his hand. "Be assured that I do. It is a matter of honor between gentlemen, but you cannot prevent me from being alarmed at the prospect."

"And you may be assured, dearest, that I will do nothing to provoke a confrontation with any man from now on."

"I am heartily relieved to hear you say so, and I beg your pardon if I have made a cake of myself over the matter."

"You could never be foolish in my eyes, Sophia. You are the finest female ever born."

Such high-flown praise should have pleased her more than it actually did. When she caught sight of Senorita Malliende, who had been surrounded since her arrival by admirers, she asked, "Did you, after such a disconcerting experience, find Senorita Malliende diverting when you called upon her?"

From his expression the young man appeared discomposed by the question, and then, fingering the folds of his neck cloth, he replied, "Oh, indeed."

"No doubt she was in high snuff to see you both."

"Needless to say. However, Manville and I were not the only ones present. At any time one is bound to find a procession of callers at her house. I scarce had an opportunity to exchange a word with her. I only wonder she isn't totally overset by all the fuss and botheration, but she maintains an air of sweetness even when she must be exhausted."

Sophia laughed softly. "There are few females who would take such attention amiss, Felix."

Her laughter came during a pause in the music, supplied by a very excellent orchestra. The earl, who had been dancing with Lady Whitchurch, heard it and glanced across at them. He caught Sophia's eye and she looked away quickly unable to hold his dark, fathomless gaze.

"I wonder if Lord Manville and Lady Whitchurch have renewed their close friendship," Sophia mused.

"How should I know?" Felix replied, and only then did Sophia realize she had spoken aloud.

"If anyone is to know, it will be you. There are few gentlemen as close to him as you are Felix."

"Manville has become as close as oak since his return from the Peninsula." He stood up abruptly and said, "Come, Sophia, let us join the country dance. I grow weary of this endless speculation about my cousin."

It was, Sophia reflected, the very first time she had detected peevishness in Felix's manner where his cousin was concerned, and she did wonder if he was beginning to see the earl as a man possessing human frailties, rather than the hero he had always seemed.

Throughout their quiet conversation Senorita Malliende had stood up for several of the dances, imbuing them with her own brand of grace and skill.

Sophia watched her thoughtfully as she took her own place in the set, asking, "I wonder why Senorita Malliende is able to perform our own traditional dances so well so soon after her arrival in England."

"By all accounts she has been taking lessons," her future husband replied. "Needless to say it would take her little time to become accomplished."

"Oh, needless to say," Sophia responded, her voice heavy with sarcasm, and she was rewarded by a dark look from her husband-to-be.

As was usual, Sophia enjoyed the dance, aware that she, too, had a light step. After it had ended, Felix drifted away to converse with a few of his cronies and Celia Waddell took the opportunity of accosting her friend.

"How good it is to see you and Mr. Harcourt behaving like a pair of mooncalves," Celia greeted her friend.

Sophia adjusted her paisley shawl, aware that the

earl was now standing against one of the room's pillars, his arms folded across his chest, watching her.

"No more than you and Captain Murchison, I fancy."

The young lady's face took on a look of petulance. "You could not be more wrong, I fear."

At last Sophia gave her friend her full attention. "Oh? Have you two parted brass rags?"

"Not precisely, but Tom is being exceedingly tiresome just now. He accused me of being a flirt." Sophia could not help but smile. "Mayhap he actually believes that because we are to be married I should respond to the flattery of other gentlemen with the demeanor of a plaster statue."

"Oh, I'm persuaded Captain Murchison would not wish that for anything, Celia," Sophia replied in a sympathetic manner.

"If no one else found me fetching, Murchison would not do so either."

"It must be very provoking for you, dear," Sophia responded with a smile.

Two young bucks arrived to claim them for the very popular Scottish reel and by the time it had ended, Sophia began to feel she had been exaggerating in her mind any problems between her and Felix.

"My dear," Lady Whitchurch said breathlessly as she bore down upon Sophia, "it does my heart good to see you and Mr. Harcourt together and enjoying each other's company with such relish."

"I am most gratified to hear you say so, my lady," Sophia responded, wondering why first Celia and now Lady Whitchurch found it so worthy of comment. "We have always enjoyed a fine accord. No doubt that is why we decided to marry."

"Whenever I see young couples together, like you and Mr. Harcourt, I am happily reminded of the halcyon days of my own betrothal," the marchioness went on, heedless of Sophia's sarcasm.

On Sophia's part she was longing to ask her to which betrothal she was referring, but forbore to do so.

Lady Whitchurch opened her fan and cast a malicious eye in the direction of Senorita Malliende who was, as usual, surrounded by a knot of young admirers. "I confess," she admitted, "to admiring her footwork, which is tolerable, but I cannot for anything understand why she has become so fashionable."

"Mayhap it is her sweet disposition," Sophia ventured, aware that this comment was likely to vex the woman.

The marchioness looked at her askance. "My dear, you must be a green girl to believe a gentleman pursues on opera-dancer for the sweetness of her disposition. However, I must own, with Lady Truscott so closely chaperoning the chit, there is more to the matter than we yet know."

"I cannot conceive what that might be, my lady," Sophia answered artlessly.

The marchioness glanced toward Senorita Malliende once more. "My dear, have you not noticed how glowing she looks this evening?"

"I don't regard it out of the way, my lady. I am sure Senorita Malliende is normally radiant."

"Since she made her debut, I have observed her closely, and I assure you it is out of the ordinary.

Moreover, it is evident by the way she moves around Manville House with such sureness, she believes she will, before long, become mistress of it. There is no other explanation."

Sophia's eyes opened wide in surprise, but she wondered why she was so shocked by Lady Whitchurch's observation. The earl had gone to a great deal of trouble to bring Senorita Malliende from the Peninsula, and if he considered surrendering his bachelor status, it would only be to a female desired by many others. The talk had been of little else of late.

"You must have an opinion on the matter, Miss Kingsland," Lady Whitchurch persisted in the brittle tone that was beginning to grate on Sophia.

She remained thoughtful for a moment or two before replying in as careful a manner as she could contrive, "I believe if Lord Manville intends to make Senorita Malliende his wife, they will make a most handsome couple, but we shall all be obliged to wait patiently until they see fit to make an announcement."

The marchioness's eyes narrowed somewhat. "If that was about to happen, you would be one of the first to know, would you not, being affianced to Manville's cousin?"

"If there was anything to know, I daresay Felix would confide in me, but as he has not yet done so, we must assume nothing is decided." Sophia eyed her curiously. "If you'll forgive me for saying so, ma'am, you do seem exceptionally concerned for Lord Manville's matrimonial prospects."

"It is incumbent upon me to concern myself, Miss

Kingsland. His lordship has always been dear to me. We do remain close."

"Then it is like you would know more about his intentions than I."

Suddenly Lady Whitchurch smiled quite radiantly as she looked past Sophia. A moment later the reason for that dazzling smile became evident when the earl could be seen approaching them through a knot of guests. Aware that he was looking directly at her, Sophia opened her fan to obscure the lower part of her face.

"Manville, how odd you should approach us just now," the marchioness declared. "Miss Kingsland and I were just discussing you."

Sophia hoped that her face was hidden sufficiently to obscure the fact that her cheeks had become pink under his scrutiny and also because of the marchioness's less than diplomatic declaration.

"What an intriguing thought," he responded. "I do trust you were treating me kindly."

Lady Whitchurch tapped him playfully on the arm with her fan. "You cannot expect us to reveal the content of our coze, Manville."

"After further thought I don't believe I would wish you to do so, ma'am," he responded with a laugh.

When he looked once again at Sophia, Lady Whitchurch said quickly, putting a proprietorial hand on his arm, "Ah, the cotillion is announced. Manville, recall how we always used to dance the cotillion so well together."

"I believe I do," was his diplomatic reply.

"When we stand up together on this occasion, it will be just like it used to be."

As the marchioness drew him away, he cast Sophia a wry and apologetic look and she was left with the distinct impression she was the one with whom he wished to dance. Although she was always well supplied with partners, she couldn't help but feel a small dart of disappointment as the handsome couple took their places in the set with Lady Whitchurch laughing and flirting in her usual outrageous manner.

"How honored I am that you have found time to stand up with me on two occasions this evening," she told him.

"Do I detect a note of censure in your voice, Merinda?" he responded.

"That would be churlish of me, indeed." She glanced to where Senorita Malliende was standing. "I daresay you are well occupied of late with your . . . protégée."

"Among others."

"Really, Manville, you are being very provoking. We once so enjoyed each other's company, but now I see you only on occasions such as this. Do you intend to marry her?"

The earl appeared to remain good humored. "You know better than to ask such a question, Merinda."

The marchioness made a noise that indicated her annoyance. "I know you well enough to concede there must be a female involved. There always used to be and you made no attempt to hide her."

"Once, I enjoyed every pursuit in the full view of anyone who wished to observe. I confess, I have since learned better."

She tapped him playfully with her fan. "Admit you are intent upon punishing me."

"Not in the least, my dear. Why should I?"

"Then tell me you still do not care for me," she teased.

He smiled. "So, you have rumbled the secret I have tried so hard to contain." When she cast him a look of outrage, he went on in a far gentler tone, "You are incredibly lovely and a prodigious wit, but one quality I value above those is loyalty, which I fear is the one thing you do not possess."

Lady Whitchurch gasped and looked furious. Fortunately the dance began, making conversation impossible and the couple appeared an ideal pair to all those observing them with so much interest.

Twelve

As Lord Manville and Lady Whitchurch went onto the dance floor, one of Sophia's erstwhile suitors indicated from across the room that he wished to dance with her, and as she went to join him, she glimpsed Celia in laughing conversation with young Viscount Latham. She could not help but suppress a sigh, especially as it was very evident that the girl had liberally dampened her petticoats so that her gown clung all the more to her ample curves.

When the cotillion finished, Sophia went in search of Felix, for she was convinced he wished to dance the quadrille with her. However, before she could catch sight of him, Senorita Malliende broke away from those with whom she was in light-hearted conversation and arrested Sophia's progression through the crowds.

"Miss Kingsland, how unfortunate we have not

yet had an opportunity to converse this evening. I had so much looked forward to doing so."

"Senorita Malliende, you have been very well occupied since your arrival. You are much in demand, which is not so surprising."

"It is to me!" The young woman laughed. "I continue to be astounded by my success, I assure you."

"You should not be. Your talent is prodigious."

The young woman looked wry. "In all truth, Lord Manville always assured me it would be so."

Sophia smiled sweetly. "He is so rarely wrong about anything, don't you find?"

"I am so glad we are of one accord on that score, Miss Kingsland. There are those who, I have discovered, do not think too kindly of his lordship, mainly because of some harmless caprices in his youth, which are common to all young bucks and do not signify at all. I am fully aware that you, Miss Kingsland, as well as Mr. Harcourt, share my admiration for Lord Manville."

"I cannot think why you should consider me his champion," Sophia answered, wondering if Lady Whitchurch might be correct after all.

It could well be that Senorita Malliende's insistence upon singing the earl's praises at every turn indicated something more than mere friendship between them.

"I am fully aware that in English society one must not be too enthusiastic about anyone or anything. It is not fashionable, but you cannot fail to admire much in him."

Fortunately Sophia was not called upon to reply, for at that moment Lady Whitchurch passed by on the arm of Lord Smythe, and Manuela Malliende's smile faded as the marchioness nodded curtly in their direction.

"What a tiresome female," Senorita Malliende confided and Sophia looked at her with interest. "Every time we meet, she insists upon informing me of some aspect of her betrothal to Lord Manville. I cannot conceive why she should imagine that is of any interest to me. It is my earnest opinion that his lordship was most fortunate in escaping the clutches of that creature."

"Once again I am inclined to agree with you, senorita. It is only to be hoped that Lord Manville is also sensible of his good fortune."

"Of what particular good fortune should I be sensible?" asked the earl, coming up behind the two young ladies, causing Sophia to start.

Manuela Malliende's face was again transformed into a brilliant smile. "It is of no account," she told him. "This is a brilliant squeeze, my lord."

"It is most gratifying to hear you say so."

"No doubt many others must have expressed similar sentiments this evening," Sophia told him.

He smiled. "They most certainly have, but it is possible what everyone is enjoying is the novelty of the occasion, Miss Kingsland."

"Well then, you must ensure it does not remain an unusual event," she responded.

"Miss Kingsland, I am inclined to agree with you."

Manuela Malliende beamed at them, not at all put out that Sophia was monopolizing his attention, which indicated she did, indeed, possess a sweet nature. All at once Sophia wished she had good reason to dislike her, but in all conscience she could not.

"May I have the honor of standing up with you for the quadrille, Miss Kingsland?' he asked, a moment later.

Once again she experienced a perplexing amount of regret. "Oh, I believe I am engaged to dance with Felix on this occasion."

"That cannot be," the other woman said in some consternation. "It is the quadrille, is it not?"

"It is," Sophia answered.

"Then I am the one who is engaged to stand up with Mr. Harcourt."

Forestalling any further argument, Felix joined them at that moment. He was looking eager to participate in the quadrille and all his attention was focused upon the dancer.

Without uttering another word, Sophia turned on her heel and walked onto the dance floor, followed by the earl.

He looked somewhat concerned. "I believe you must blame me for the confusion, Miss Kingsland."

"I cannot conceive how that can be, my lord," she answered, somewhat coolly.

"Earlier this evening when conversing with Felix, I indicated a wish to stand up with you, but doubted any of your dances would be free. He kindly offered the quadrille to me, which I considered a great sacrifice on his part."

Sophia could only smile at such an evident untruth, but she was amazed that he even troubled to try and prevent any possible quarrel between her and Felix. This was one side to his character few people had been privileged to see.

"One of Felix's most endearing qualities is his generosity, my lord," she answered, and he looked much relieved.

Although the earl had displayed some considerable concern for Sophia's feelings, the same could not be said, however, for Felix, who looked blissfully unaware of causing any discord over the matter of with whom he should stand up. When the dance ended, Sophia was only sorry it could not have lasted longer, for she had decided the quadrille was by far her favorite dance.

"You may be certain, Miss Kingsland, that I shall not be so tardy in engaging you for one of the sets on future occasions," the earl told her.

"You should not trouble your head on the matter, for I am sure Felix can always be persuaded to surrender his turn."

He looked amused and she was certain he knew she had not been hoodwinked by his clumsy excuse on Felix's behalf. She only admired his effort to set the matter to rights.

As he escorted her back to the edge of the floor, they both suddenly became aware of a very tense atmosphere nearby where a crowd had gathered. Both Sophia and the earl looked across with interest to see Captain Murchison and Lord Latham facing each other, their features livid with anger.

"Name your seconds and I will meet you whenever you please," Captain Murchison challenged, and Sophia gasped in alarm.

Unthinkingly she put her hand on the earl's arm and squeezed it hard as she whispered, "Oh, my goodness."

"You are acting like a pair of chuckleheads,"

Celia Waddell cried, much to the amusement of those witnessing the confrontation. "I demand that you both cease this foolishness."

"This is none of your concern, Miss Waddell," Lord Latham told her. "Be pleased to stand aside."

Celia Waddell stamped her foot on the floor. "It is most certainly a matter of my concern."

"By your leave, Miss Kingsland," the earl excused himself and grim-faced he pushed his way forward.

Almost without thinking, Sophia pressed forward in his wake, seeing that her friend was wide-eyed with terror at what was afoot.

"Gentlemen," the earl addressed them in a calm yet authoritative manner, "I believe we can resolve this the better in private."

As Celia was shaking convulsively, Sophia went to put her arm around her friend's shoulders while the three grim-faced gentlemen strode out of the ballroom. A great burst of chattering followed their departure as everyone began to discuss the altercation.

"What the devil has happened?" Felix asked, coming late to the furor.

Manuela Malliende was still accompanying him, but all Sophia's concern was for her friend just then. "In truth I am not sure," she answered as Celia hurried out of the ballroom. "Excuse me, I beg of you, but I must go to Miss Waddell."

She hurried out after Celia, who was found dabbing at her eyes in the hall outside. Sophia led her to a sofa in an alcove away from the amused stares of the other guests.

"Don't get into such a pucker over this," Sophia

urged as Celia twisted a damp handkerchief in her hands.

"It is all my fault, even though Tom accused Lord Latham of trifling with me. If they fight a duel, I shall never be able to forgive myself."

"Faddle!" Sophia teased. "It is most unlike Captain Murchison to want to call a gentleman out."

"He was urged on by that vile Lord Smythe. I'd as lief Tom call *him* out!"

"Have no fear, Celia," her friend assured her, "Lord Manville will persuade them not to follow such a foolish course. It will soon be resolved to everyone's satisfaction."

"That is my fear! Lord Manville has always been foremost in encouraging such matters to proceed, as everyone knows."

"Not any longer. You will see very shortly that I am correct, but, Celia, you must from now on resolve to behave in a more responsible manner. You are, after all, betrothed to Captain Murchison. You will be obliged to decide whether you wish to marry him or continue to play the flirt."

"You are scarce qualified to lecture me," the girl said resentfully, "after all I have observed of late."

"What ... do you mean?" asked Sophia, rather taken aback.

"Since your betrothal you have been observed in Lord Manville's company almost as much as that of Mr. Harcourt."

On hearing this allegation, Sophia immediately became flustered. "I do not like your inference, Celia, even though in your current mood of despondency I hesitate to reprove you for it."

"I am the most disagreeable creature who ever

lived," Miss Waddell declared, giving in once again to self-pity. "I do not deserve your friendship, and it would be entirely justified if you were to cast me off."

Sophia was then forced to smile, despite her feeling of disquiet. "If I have been making myself amiable toward Lord Manville, there has been a very good reason to do so."

Celia looked disbelieving. "The reason being you are as wicked a flirt as I, only Felix Harcourt is not like to call his cousin out!"

"I am beginning to be out of all patience with you, Celia, and I am very much afraid I shall be obliged to explain matters to you, although in truth I am loath to do so. You are such a tattle-box."

"Only about others," she protested, drawing a look of disbelief from Sophia. "On this occasion I assure you, you may rely upon my discretion."

Sophia drew a deep sigh, aware that she might soon come to regret speaking, but all the same, feeling she must justify what others could interpret as coquettish behavior.

"There is quite a simple explanation I assure you." Miss Waddell looked at her with the utmost interest. "When Lord Manville first returned to London, we took each other in dislike—at least I did. His lordship intimated he thought Felix too young to consider matrimony, which I took amiss."

"I am not surprised!"

"In any event the situation was making Felix miserable, so I resolved to be more pleasant to his cousin, who is in fact as close as a brother."

"That is an exceedingly long explanation," Celia remarked, sniffling loudly.

"Nevertheless I can vouch for the veracity of it. It is not a Banbury Tale, you may be certain."

The coze between the two young ladies was interrupted by the arrival of Captain Murchison, who, from his chastened expression, evidently wished to make amends for his foolhardy behavior.

Diplomatically Sophia left them to their reconciliation and returned to the ballroom.

The first person she saw was Lady Truscott, who immediately asked, "Is Miss Waddell recovered?"

"Yes, indeed, and it is all due to Lord Manville that a dreadful scandal has been averted."

"I can scarce believe it of him!" his aunt admitted. "There are moments, Miss Kingsland, when I wonder if it is, indeed, the same man who went to the Peninsula with Wellington. The other Manville would not have discouraged the duel."

"Be certain he has done so now."

"I am most relieved." Lady Truscott shook her head smilingly. "Young people are ever foolish, my dear. I am not so far removed from my own youth to recall it is so."

When she drifted away into the crowds, Sophia once more found herself being approached by the earl.

"That is the second time today you have averted a duel, which is the oddest thing to me," she told him. "You was always used to be perpetrator of such meetings, if all I have been told is true."

"I cannot deny it, but mayhap my experience in the Peninsula showed me the futility of all manner of conflict."

"I am persuaded you suffered greatly," she said

in a soft tone, her eyes clouding at the thought of it.

"You must not allow it to trouble your head, for it is of no account any longer. Much good has come out of it." Before she could ask him what he meant, he went on, "Tell me, Miss Kingsland, will you do me the honor of riding with me on the morrow."

Sophia was surprised and it was several moments before she could answer, "I believed you to be going racing with Felix tomorrow."

The earl looked wry. "I have cried off that particular engagement. Felix is being accompanied by a few of his cronies, and to one of my advanced years they seem scarce out of leading strings."

Sophia could not help but laugh, but underneath there was an underlying feeling of unease, for her husband-to-be had seemed rather young to her, too, of late.

"His behavior this afternoon certainly gives strength to that belief."

"You must not continue to let it tease you, Miss Kingsland." The concern in his manner, the anxiety in his eyes, caused her heart to flutter unevenly. "I shall call for you on the morrow," he added without waiting for her acceptance of his invitation.

His eyes seemed to hold hers captive in their dark, fathomless depths, and she could not draw her gaze away from his until her own mother's voice caused her to turn on her heel.

Feeling somewhat bemused, she heard Lady Kingsland say, "What a splendid hurricane, my lord. In the future you must arrange a diversion with far more regularity than in the past!"

"It will be my pleasure, ma'am," was his urbane reply, and it was as if the moment between them had never happened.

Thirteen

"Why are you going out riding with Lord Manville?" Jessica asked as her sister hovered nervously on the landing the following afternoon. "Surely you should be going with Felix."

Dressed in a blue velvet pelisse with black frogging and a matching poke-brimmed bonnet, Sophia glanced frequently out of a first floor window that overlooked the street.

"Why should I not ride with Felix's cousin if I am asked?" she responded, affecting a haughty air.

"It seems a trifle odd to me that is all, now you are affianced. Does not Felix mind?"

"Felix is gone to the races, and in any event he is more than anxious for me to have an amiable relationship with Lord Manville. We have not always been of one accord."

"And now you are?"

"I did not precisely say that," Sophia answered, unable to keep the irritation out of her voice.

"I should have thought it might have been more fitting for you to curry favor with Lady Truscott, who is a formidable lady, by all accounts, and exceedingly influential."

"Stuff and nonsense!" Sophia retorted. "Lady Truscott has always been most condescending to me."

"So has Lord Manville, from all I have observed."

"Faddle!" was her sister's uncompromising reply. "You know nothing of the matter."

"I am beginning to realize the truth of that," Jessica agreed at last.

Sophia shrank back from the window when she saw the earl's curricle drawing up outside. She watched him climb down, looking as elegant as always in his caped driving coat and high-crowned beaver hat. He handed the ribbons to his tiger and then entered the hall.

Watching from the upper landing, Sophia heard him say, "Pray inform Miss Sophia Kingsland that the Earl of Manville is here. She is expecting me."

"Gentlemen calling is just as it used to be for the short while before Felix came up to scratch," Jessica said gleefully to be rewarded by an icy look from her sister.

When the house steward came up the stairs to deliver the earl's message, Sophia dallied some few minutes more.

"I don't consider it wise to keep someone as toplofty as Lord Manville cooling his heels," Jessica ventured.

"Nor does it do to exhibit too much eagerness toward any gentleman," her sister responded. "You would do very well to learn that before your come out, Jessica. No one will value your company if it is too readily available."

"But surely that is of no account in this instance," the girl answered eyeing her slyly, "for you are already engaged to marry Felix and you are going riding with his cousin."

Sophia did not trouble to answer. At this point she started to walk down the stairs to see him examining a portrait of one of her ancestors that was hanging in the hall. When she was halfway down the stairs, he turned on his heel and saw her.

His dark eyes seemed to take in every aspect of her appearance, which was a discomforting experience for Sophia, but she continued down the stairs, appearing more composed than she truly was. No one looking at her could have discerned the sudden feeling of panic which assailed her the moment he had turned to look at her.

He came to meet her at the foot of the stairs. Taking her hand and raising it to his lips, he said, "Miss Kingsland, you look utterly delightful."

A faint shade of pink tinged her cheeks. "A compliment from the notoriously particular Earl of Manville is praise indeed."

"With you sitting at my side, Miss Kingsland, my reputation for being punctilious in my choice of female companionship will be upheld. I only trust that my cousin will enjoy his day at the races as much as I will delight in the company of his bride-to-be."

Now Sophia's cheeks grew even more pink. "Indeed he will, especially if he returns having won his wagers."

"Knowing Felix as I do, he is more like to return with his pockets to let."

"You are not the best influence on him, my lord," she teased gently.

"I must own that is so."

"And you have been a great deal in each other's company since you returned."

The earl looked surprised. "Not as often as you might suppose, Miss Kingsland. He now has a most delightful future bride with whom he quite understandably wishes to be."

He led her out to the waiting curricle and as he handed her up to the box, his eyes met hers once again. " 'Tis amazing!" he declared. "The color of your bonnet matches exactly that of your eyes."

Sophia looked startled and a moment later he came round to take his seat beside her. With the tiger ensconced in the basket, the earl took up the ribbons and the carriage set off. As it did so, Sophia glanced up at the house to see Jessica's grinning face at the window.

"Has Miss Waddell recovered from her megrims of last night?" he asked as they drove out of Manchester Square.

"I believe it safe to say that she and Captain Murchison are reconciled."

"That is splendid news."

Pushing her hands into her muff, Sophia allowed herself a quick glance at his aquiline features as he concentrated on maneuvering through the crush of vehicles on the road.

"It was kind of you to be so concerned. They owe you a great debt of gratitude."

"You must not give me too much credit, Miss Kingsland, for what I did was born of a selfish desire. I did not want a challenge to be issued and taken up in my house."

"I cannot understand why that would concern you overmuch, my lord."

He cast her a smiling glance. "Had they fought that duel, the only thing that would have remained uppermost in everyone's mind was the fact it had happened in my house. Before a day or two had passed, the fault would have been attributed quite firmly to me."

"Do you truly care about that?" she asked, eyeing him with true curiosity.

"It seems that I do, ma'am."

"From all Felix has told me of you, I am most surprised to hear you say so."

He looked amused. "What *has* Felix told you about me?"

Sophia laughed. "Things which, I regret to say, would alarm any young lady."

"Yet you are trustful enough to agree to ride with me today. That is exceedingly brave of you, ma'am."

"Mayhap I enjoy flirting with danger."

"From all I have observed in *you*, I take leave to doubt it, but that does infer that I am a dangerous person, which I most heartily deny!"

"In any event, I am surely not the only female ever to go riding with you. I am persuaded I am only one of very many."

"Oh, you may be certain that my life is now much

more mundane since my return to England," he told her laughingly.

They were driving along the Marylebone Road and Sophia realized then that they were traveling toward Marylebone Park and not Hyde Park, which was more usual. However, she had long since acknowledged that the earl was not a man easy to categorize.

A column of soldiers was marching down the road and it was not until they passed that Sophia said, "Senorita Malliende must be very much looking forward to dancing at Carlton House."

"I believe it would be more accurate to say she is apprehensive, and who can blame her?"

"Not I, although I'm persuaded she will treat the engagement as diligently as any other."

"There is no doubt in my mind she will be a triumph, as is usual."

As the curricle passed through the park gates, Sophia felt a trifle miffed to hear such fulsome praise pass his lips, even though she would have expected nothing else.

"You will, of course, be present on that evening," he continued.

"I would not wish to miss it for anything. I am greatly honored by the invitation."

He laughed then, quite unexpectedly. "You need not be, Miss Kingsland, for it will be a horrendous squeeze."

"You must forgive my childish and unfashionable enthusiasm, my lord," she answered, very much on her dignity, "but the function is a novelty to me."

"And I am jaded! You need not say so, for I know it!"

Sophia found her own lips quirking into a smile. Here in the park he could afford not to concentrate on driving so much and was able to cast her a smile that was calculated to banish any small irritation she was feeling.

It was not so fashionable to ride in Marylebone Park, so it was nowhere near as crowded as Hyde Park. Their ride there would have been interrupted by constant calls from acquaintances. It gave Sophia no small amount of pleasure to reflect he might have chosen Marylebone Park just because they could enjoy each other's company the better.

"So you own that you find the Season dull," she teased, her eyes sparkling with mischief.

"I own that I *thought* I might," he admitted, "but quite the contrary has been true. I find I am enjoying myself far more than at any time before that I can recall."

"The astonishing success of Senorita Malliende has no doubt contributed to that," she ventured, gazing at him thoughtfully.

His expression gave nothing away. "That is, I own, a distinct possibility."

"You must be crying roast meat to have judged her ability so well."

"I cannot claim so much credit, Miss Kingsland, but it is true that both she and I are quite astonished at the extent of her popularity, both on a professional and personal level."

"How fortunate she is to have met you."

"Oh no, Miss Kingsland, I assure you quite the contrary is true."

177

Sophia had little time to ponder on the meaning of his words, for she had caught sight of a familiar yellow phaeton coming toward them. At first she thought she might have been mistaken in her identity of it, but then her eyes narrowed as she watched it coming closer.

Suddenly she drew in a sharp breath when she finally recognized for certain that is was, indeed, Felix's phaeton and his familiar figure was tooling the ribbons. The female at his side was no less familiar to her. She was well-known to almost every member of the *ton*, but Sophia was still assailed by a feeling of unreality on seeing Felix riding with Manuela Malliende in Marylebone Park.

The moment she actually realized it was Felix and the dancer, she could not repress a gasp of dismay, for she had been so certain he was engaged to go racing with his cronies that day. It was then that the earl saw his cousin and his expression hardened.

With consummate skill he directed his team in another direction so that there should be no embarrassing confrontation. When the phaeton passed by at a reasonable distance, Felix and the opera-dancer were so engrossed in their lighthearted conversation, they did not notice the other, distinctive, carriage and its occupants going fast in the opposite direction.

While the earl's curricle headed toward the gates of the park at a spanking pace, Sophia's mind was in a turmoil. Seeing the couple together was, naturally, totally unexpected, and it was evident they must have chosen Marylebone Park in order not to be seen by others. Sophia had attributed the earl's choice to just such a reason, and she had even been flattered by it, but she was well aware that any young buck fortunate enough to be escorting Manuela Malliende at the height of her popularity would wish everyone to witness it.

"Miss Kingsland," ventured the earl at last as the curricle bowled along Marylebone Road, "you must not be overset by what you saw. It is of no real consequence."

Sophia raised her eyes slowly to meet his and he could not possibly mistake the misery he saw there. However, he was not to know, as she did, that the cause of her pain was not the sight of Felix and Manuela Malliende enjoying each other's company so evidently. Her anguish was based upon what she believed to be the earl's hand in the matter.

From the first she had doubted his honor, but then had come to trust him. Now, she recognized her initial distrust had been wise after all. He was a devil, and all the more dangerous for appearing so bland.

"Miss Kingsland," he persisted in the face of her continued silence, "I beg of you not to take this to heart."

She turned on him then. "I have it in mind taking it to heart is precisely what you wish me to do."

His look of shock and surprise greatly satisfied her for she did not doubt he hoped to appear the innocent in the matter. He probably considered her a numskull who would put all the blame upon Felix and not fathom his part in today's charade.

"I cannot conceive what you may mean, ma'am, although I do perceive you are overset. I do not doubt for one moment my cousin will have a satisfactory explanation for today's events."

"Why don't you have the grace to own that you knew Felix would be riding with Senorita Malliende at the very time we would be passing through Marylebone Park? Is that not precisely why you took me there?"

"Miss Kingsland, I admit nothing of the kind. As far as I was aware, Felix had gone to Epsom with some of his cronies as arranged earlier." His tone had become noticeably cold. To some it would have been worrying, but to Sophia it merely underlined what she believed. "I cannot conceive why you should think I would wish to vex you so."

"Because you have always, yes always, disapproved of our betrothal."

"Miss Kingsland . . ."

"You considered Felix too young for matrimony and mayhap after our first encounter, the one in Leeke Lane, you thought me unsuited to your cousin. Whatever your reason, if one of us cries off that will suit you perfectly, for you would not wish to be proved wrong about us."

"Miss Kingsland, I really must protest!"

"It is of no account to me if you do. I am entirely to blame for not recognizing the danger you presented right from the outset. At least I did, only I allowed your flummery to make a cake of me. You, no doubt, believe I have windmills in my head and you are entirely correct! I think you are the most odious man I have ever had the misfortune to meet!"

Sophia was very close to breaking down in tears at this point and it was a great relief to her when the carriage drew up outside her house. Without waiting for him to come around and help her from the carriage, she climbed down herself. However, the curricle had been built primarily for speed rather than comfort and, being unused to it, she stumbled in her haste to escape his odious company and landed instead in an undignified heap on the ground.

It was the last straw and by the time the earl had reached her, the tears were flowing freely down her cheeks. Despite the trimming to which she had just subjected him, his face was a picture of concern for her.

"Miss Kingsland," he said in shocked tones, brushing aside the lackey, who would have come to her assistance.

He helped her to her feet, exhibiting great concern, and as he did so, he cradled her close to him and momentarily Sophia gave into the impulse of staying in his arms. A moment later, however, he stepped back, almost abruptly.

"My dear Miss Kingsland—Sophia—are you hurt?" he asked and the concern in his manner, which she knew masked his contempt of her, cut her like a knife.

Mute with misery she shook her head and made an absentminded attempt to brush the dust off her pelisse. He produced a handkerchief, which she accepted to dab at her cheeks, and she was at once assailed by the scent of his eau de cologne.

"I do beg your pardon for making such a cake of myself," she murmured, aware that he continued to watch her with concern.

His face relaxed somewhat then. "I am sorry the

afternoon has turned out so badly. There is nothing I can do to salvage it, but I do beg you to believe I did not plan anything that happened."

He looked at her hopefully and Sophia longed to believe him, but all her instincts told her she could not. After a moment or two his look of hopefulness disappeared and his eyes grew cold once again. There was something about his expression that made her afraid.

"It seems there is nothing further to say except to thank you for your company this afternoon. Good day to you, Miss Kingsland."

As he climbed back onto the box of the curricle, Sophia was assailed by the sudden temptation to call him back and beg his pardon, but in truth she had not believed him and she merely watched in mute misery as he drove away from her without a backward glance. The fragrant handkerchief, now grubby and creased, was still clutched in her hand.

Fourteen

It was with no real relish that Sophia prepared to attend the Prince Regent's ball at Carlton House. As Lily helped her dress, Sophia reflected that she no longer had any reason to look forward to the eagerly awaited function.

She wished pride would allow her to plead a headache, but crying off this evening's function would only postpone an inevitable confrontation with those whom she believed had betrayed her. Of all three, Sophia felt least resentment toward Manuela Malliende, whom, she was sure, was innocent of any guile, and poor Felix would not even realize that his cousin was manipulating him.

"Considering where you are going and whom you are like to meet there, you look as melancholy as a gib cat," Jessica observed from her perch on the four-poster bed.

"Oh, do hold your tiresome tongue," her sister

told her, not in the least indulgent of her on this occasion.

"I do wonder why Felix Harcourt wishes to become leg-shackled to a Friday-faced creature like you."

"When you have your own circle of admirers, Jess, you will then be able to criticize me, but not before that."

"If Lord Manville had asked me to ride with him, *I* should be crying roast meat. Indeed, any debutante would."

"In my opinion that would be exceedingly unseemly, but I fear you will always act the hoyden," Sophia said, casting her sister a dark look.

"You don't intend to cry off your betrothal, do you?" Jessica asked, eyeing her anxiously.

As Lily fastened her into her peach silk gown embroidered with pearls, Sophia cast her sister a sharp look. "Why should you even think of such a thing?"

The girl shrugged slightly. "When you first became acquainted with Felix, your feelings were never in doubt, but nowadays you never act the mooncalf. It is more like you suffer a vexation of spirit."

Sophia smiled with relief. "What a foolish chit you are," she chided. "As if I would be so unfashionable."

She looked uncertain again as Lily placed Lady Truscott's pearl diadem onto her carefully arranged curls. The diadem seemed all at once the symbol of the Harcourt/Manville families, and she suddenly resented that.

"I believe I shall wear the beaded headband instead," she decided, removing the diadem quickly.

"But, ma'am," the abigail protested.

"Fetch the beaded headband, Lily, and put the diadem back in my jewel box."

The maidservant cast her mistress a worried look, but answered obligingly, "Yes, ma'am, if that is what you wish."

"It is."

Sophia cast her sister a challenging look, but for once Jessica said nothing. When the abigail went to do her mistress's bidding, the young girl said then, "If you were to cry off your wedding, it would play old Harry with my own come out."

Sophia drew a deep sigh. "You need have no concern on that score, dearest. I cannot conceive why you should think anything is amiss between us."

She brushed rouge onto her cheeks with a hare's foot and smeared red pomatum onto her lips. As she sprinkled lavender water freely about her person, she recalled that Lord Manville's handkerchief was still in one of the drawers in her dressing table. She could not for anything imagine why she had not consigned it to one of the servants for laundering and eventual return to the earl, but she made no attempt to do so, even now.

The Kingsland party eventually arrived at Carlton House after a slow and tedious journey, despite taking care to leave in good time. The protracted journey did nothing to soothe Sophia's sensibilities and for the main part of the time she remained lost in her own thoughts while her mother prattled on inanely.

As the Kingsland barouche took its turn to stop in front of the entrance to Carlton House, Sir Magnus remarked, "I would dearly like to be His Royal Highness's chandler."

"No, you would not," his wife contradicted, "for it is certain you would never be paid. You know full well Prinny is always in dun territory."

Lackeys in splendid livery assisted the ladies from the carriage. Sophia thought she would be nervous of meeting the Prince, but found herself more apprehensive of seeing Felix, for she had no notion how she should approach him on the subject of his secret ride with Manuela Malliende. The events of that particular afternoon had been going round in her head, but she still could make no sense of them.

The Prince looked rather awe inspiring, his portly figure clad in the dress uniform of a field marshall and the garter star at his breast. Ever since Wellington had begun his successful campaign in the Peninsula, the Prince had taken to wearing a military uniform whenever he appeared in public.

Lord Hertford was hovering discreetly in the background just as he had since the Prince had first taken up with the marchioness. Sophia considered him to be in an awkward situation, for he could scarce rail against his future king even if he felt inclined to do so.

As was to be expected, Carlton House was all splendor. The entrance hall had huge columns of porphyry, hundreds of candles burned in crystal chandeliers and sconces. Sophia was much impressed by the thickness of the velvet carpets, which were patterned with the Prince of Wales's feathers.

As she passed through the various salons, it became apparent that the Prince's reputation as a spendthrift was not idly earned. No expense had been spared in making Carlton House a most splendid place, and from all Sophia had heard, the Prince was doing precisely the same thing at his Marine Pavilion in Brighton.

Most of the guests were particular to make their way to admire the Prince's latest acquisition—a painting by Rembrandt, which had reputedly cost five thousand guineas.

The Prince of Wales's only child, Princess Charlotte, was also present at the ball as she was now of marriageable age. Much conversation was now centered on possible partners for this most eligible of young ladies. However, she was also as plain and as plump as her mother, Princess Caroline, who the Prince Regent could not abide, but for once the princess smiled at frequent intervals and looked rather less miserable than was usual for her.

"Don't you think Princess Charlotte looks unusually happy this evening?" Sophia asked her mother.

"I am reliably informed that His Highness has been trying to make a match between her and the Prince of Orange."

"Oh, he is a pasty-faced creature. I do not like the look of him at all."

"Nor did Her Highness, by all accounts, and that is why she is so happy tonight." Sophia looked at her curiously. "Now that Boney is defeated at Leipzig, the Prince of Orange is returning to Holland, and I have no doubt she is delighted at the news. Ah, there is Felix in conversation with Byron, of all people, and Lady Oxford. Do you know she is older than I, whereas he . . ."

Just then Sophia was not listening to her mother.

When she saw Felix with the celebrated poet and his latest paramour, she realized it had been Lord Manville she had been eager to see, despite the manner in which they had parted the last time they met.

Lord Byron looked more relaxed than was usual for him, and Sophia couldn't help but wonder if that was because Caroline Lamb had left London and was not likely to cause any more embarrassing scenes, which had delighted the *ton* and outraged those closest to the couple. Lady Oxford was evidently a calming influence on the poet genius.

The moment he caught sight of her, Felix excused himself and came to greet her. Lady Kingsland waited for only a few moments before going off in the direction of a group of her friends. Just one glance at him told Sophia he was in something of a taking.

"The devil take it, Sophia," he said, drawing her into a quiet alcove where they could converse in relative privacy. "I've been obliged to endure a dreadful trimming from Manville."

Sophia looked the picture of innocence. "Oh? On what score, Felix?"

"It seems I was seen by you and he when I was riding in Marylebone Park with Senorita Malliende."

"Oh, yes, indeed. I had almost forgotten. You were so rapt in each other's company you did not see us when we rode by."

"I cannot credit why he was angered by such an innocent act."

"Mayhap it had something to do with the fact

you had declared your intention of going to Epsom."

"Oh yes, that was certainly my original plan, but
Dickie Fensham developed an ague, Augie Pym declared he was all done up, and Freddie Allsopp was
called to his mother's bedside. Before we invited
any further ill fortune, Algy Norton and I decided
to cry off."

"You may be sure you do not have to explain the
situation to me, Felix," she answered, fanning herself furiously.

"It is a relief to hear you say so, for Manville
gave me to understand you were miffed, but dash
it all, Sophia, my riding with Senorita Malliende
was no more underhand than you and my coz."

"It really is of no account, Felix," she assured
him, belatedly recognizing the truth of what he had
said.

"That is precisely what I have been trying to impress upon my cousin. In truth, Sophia, I believe he
has been unhinged by his suffering in the war.
There is no other explanation."

Sophia played with her fan as she said breathlessly, "I have been giving the matter of our wedding a good deal of thought of late . . ."

His eyes opened wide with alarm. "Oh . . . ?"

"Why don't we arrange it to take place sooner
than we originally planned, rather than waiting
until the end of the Season?"

He smiled faintly. "When we discussed this matter at the outset it was you, as I recall, who suggested we wait until after the Season is ended, and
I was in full agreement with you. If we rush into

matrimony now, it would only give rise to a deal of tattle."

Sophia smiled faintly herself. "Mayhap the tattle-baskets will say we were much too in love to wait any longer."

He laughed without mirth. "I do not believe they would be so kind."

"Felix, will you kiss me?" she asked abruptly.

Once again he looked shocked. "What?"

"Kiss me, Felix."

"Here?" He glanced around, looking most uncomfortable. "In front of everyone?"

"No one can readily see us."

A faint flush crept into his cheeks in marked contrast to the pristine whiteness of his shirt collar, the points of which almost touched his ears. Once Sophia had considered him extremely elegant, but she realized at long last that whatever else the earl had taught him, it was certainly not his own brand of sartorial elegance.

Continuing to look discomforted by her request, he leaned forward and allowed his lips to brush hers briefly before he took her hand, saying, "Come, let us stand up for this reel, even though it is bound to be a most dreadful squeeze."

Sophia found herself being hurried onto the floor where the set was being led by the Prince Regent himself. As she automatically danced the steps to the reel, she wondered if Felix had displayed an uncharacteristic enthusiasm for dancing just to end their conversation, which had evidently discomposed him.

After the reel was over, she was immediately claimed for the following dance by a former admirer. Through the crowds she glimpsed Celia with Captain Murchison and she was glad to note all now appeared to be well with the couple. It seemed odd that Celia and her future husband were happily settled while she and Felix were now at odds. Until very recently Sophia would never have considered her own emotional well-being to be at risk.

However much she told herself Felix was the same man with whom she had fallen in love during the summer, sadly she acknowledged it was not so. Moreover, the change was not only on his part; she felt she, too, was quite a different person to the one who had naively accepted his offer of marriage. The situation was, to say the least, an awkward one and she could not see a satisfactory outcome for either of them.

Some time later when she was conversing with a group of acquaintances, Senorita Malliende's dancing display was announced. All the guests immediately made their way to an adjoining salon where rows of gilded chairs had been set out.

The Prince, flanked by Princess Charlotte and Lady Hertford, was seated at the front of the gathering and the mainly female guests on the other chairs. Many of the gentlemen stood around the perimeter of the room, which was crowded after everyone was assembled inside.

At some stage during the evening Sophia had lost sight of Felix, but now as she glanced around the room for him, instead she found herself looking directly at Lord Manville, who was standing at the back of the room. Their eyes met briefly and then Sophia averted her gaze, but not before he had nodded unsmilingly in her direction.

Sophia inclined her head slightly in response to his acknowledgment, whereupon the young lady sitting next to her asked, "What is Lord Manville really like, Miss Kingsland? Do tell. I have not had the pleasure of exchanging as much as a word with him as yet, although I am longing to do so. Everyone is in a fidge to know if he is really as wild as it is said, and you have been privileged to be in his company so often of late."

" 'Tis impossible to know what he is truly like," Sophia replied, her voice tinged with sadness. "Even Felix confesses to finding him an enigma."

"Do you know what his true relationship is with Senorita Malliende? No one seems to be sure."

"I have no more notion than anyone else. Lord Manville is one to keep his cards close to his chest." Then she added in a bitter note, "It appears to be a family trait."

The young lady looked disappointed by the answer, and Sophia was relieved of the necessity of replying to any more questions on the subject of Lord Manville by the striking up of the orchestra. A ripple of excitement spread around the audience and then Senorita Malliende appeared to begin her dance.

As always she danced enchantingly. Sophia could not hide her own admiration and admitted to herself that Manuela Malliende was entitled to the approval of the beau monde. As the distinguished audience applauded the first part of the program, Sophia caught sight of Felix at last and he was showing his admiration in a most enthusiastic manner. At one point when Senorita Malliende sank into a deep curtsy, it seemed to Sophia that she meant it just for him.

When the second part of the entertainment commenced, Sophia was left feeling even more uncomfortable. The audience continued to be entranced by the dancer, and it appeared only she was not fully attending to the entertainment until the girl suddenly faltered, tripped, and fell in an ungainly heap on the floor.

The audience cried out in dismay, the music died away abruptly and all was in confusion for a short while. Most of the audience rose to its feet and after a moment's stunned silence several people dashed forward to her aid, foremost among them was Felix Harcourt.

Unthinkingly Sophia pressed forward, too. She could see that Manuela Malliende's face was creased with pain as pandemonium reigned around her. The Prince was giving orders to the lackeys, but to Sophia's amazement, it was Felix who very gently lifted the dancer into his arms and began to carry her to the privacy of an anteroom.

It was only what most of the other gentlemen present would have done if they'd had the presence of mind. That in itself did not alarm Sophia unduly. It was, however, the tender, loving look upon Felix's face that shocked her.

As the crowd fell back to allow them room to pass, Sophia did so, too, unable to take her eyes off Felix who, in his turn, was aware only of the girl in his arms. Fortunately no one else had noticed, nor would they have taken his gesture as anything other than gentlemanly.

When Sophia managed to drag her eyes away

from them, she found herself face-to-face with the earl, and from the pitying look in his eyes she knew he, too, had interpreted Felix's expression in the same way. Numb, she turned away, wondering what she should do, where she should go. Fortunately no one noticed her, so intent were they on discussing the unfortunate accident.

"Will she be able to dance again?" was the recurrent question on everyone's lips.

"How could one so surefooted fall in such an awkward manner?" someone else ventured.

"How dreadful that it should happen tonight, at the highest point in her life."

As the discussion took place all around her, Sophia felt a hand on her arm. When she looked up, it was to find the earl at her side.

"You look to be in need of some air, Miss Kingsland," he said and before she could argue that point, he was guiding her quickly out of the room.

Just as they left the room, they came upon Lady Whitchurch and her eyebrows rose on seeing them together. "Oh, what a dreadful thing to happen," she lamented without the slightest trace of sincerity.

"It most certainly is," the earl agreed.

The marchioness then transferred her gimlet gaze to Sophia. "How evenhanded you two gentlemen are, Manville. While your cousin is caring for Senorita Malliende you are being kind enough to escort Miss Kingsland."

"We are an exceedingly close family, ma'am," he replied with aplomb and then gently drew Sophia past her.

Unaware that the marchioness was noting their

movement with an enigmatic smile on her face, Sophia had no notion where the earl was taking her, but it was evident he knew his way around Carlton House. Very soon they came upon a deserted corridor and he seated her on a sofa, taking her fan and cooling her reddened cheeks with it.

"How do you feel now?" he asked, with so much concern she felt like giving in to the tears she had so far been forcing back.

However, she contrived to respond with a wry smile. "*I* am quite robust, I thank you, my lord. Surely your concern should be for Senorita Malliende, to whom this accident is a great blow."

"I am much concerned for her, you may be sure, but she is, as you have seen, in good hands. I overheard His Royal Highness ordering his own physician to be summoned, so she will receive the very best of attention. It is you who concerns me at present."

"I cannot for anything imagine why," she responded, affecting an air of unconcern.

"You looked so shocked. I was afraid you might swoon."

"I have never done so in my entire life!"

A spark of amusement came into his eyes as they continued to watch her carefully. "That is a great relief to me, Miss Kingsland. Forgive me my concern for you."

Sophia sat up straight and kept her eyes averted from his. "I am made of sterner stuff than you evidently believe." His lips quirked into the semblance of a smile briefly and then it was gone to be replaced by a renewal of his concern. "In any event," she continued, "I wonder you wish to concern yourself with me at all after the manner in which I addressed you the other day."

"You were overset. It was understandable, but you must not take it to heart, ma'am. Young bucks are often foolish over opera-dancers and it means little to them in reality. I have been guilty of such folly myself on occasions."

Sophia clasped her hands in a composed manner in her lap. "If we are both to be truthful, my lord, we will own that what Felix feels for Senorita Malliende is not in the usual manner of infatuation. He is not so foolish, I fear."

"What do you intend to do about it?" he asked in the gentlest of tones, which brought her close to tears again.

It was noted by Sophia that he made no attempt to argue his cousin's innocence now, something for which she was grateful.

"If we were already married, I would have no choice but to suffer the consequences of it in silence as so many others are obliged to do. As we are not married . . ."

Her voice tailed away when she realized he had moved closer to her. "Do you love him so very much, Sophia?"

It was his use of her name that caused the tears to flow at last. They trembled on her lashes as his hand caressed her cheek. A moment later when he drew her into the circle of his arms, she did not resist and when he kissed her it was as sublime as she recalled from that other brief time, only on this occasion she responded with wholehearted fervor.

At last when she laid her head on his shoulders,

she sighed, "How can I love Felix when I feel like this about you?"

Once again his lips met hers as he murmured, "I believe we have both wanted this since our first meeting."

The kisses were at once both gentle and passionate, and Sophia hoped they would never end. At last she recognized this *is* what she had wanted since the time he had come to her rescue. Only pride and fear had prevented her from acknowledging the fact.

They remained locked in one another's arms until a footstep nearby caused them to break apart rather abruptly. Sophia looked up in alarm to see Felix approaching them with a face like thunder. There was no doubt he had observed them in the kind of passionate embrace she had never enjoyed in his arms.

"So, Lady Whitchurch was correct when she said she saw you both coming in this direction."

The earl got quickly to his feet. It was the first time Sophia had seen him looking remotely discomposed. "Felix, Miss Kingsland was feeling the effects of the heat and I . . ."

The young man's face twisted into a mask of contempt. "Indeed. So, in true Manville fashion you felt it incumbent upon you to make love to her. What humbug. You could at least have the grace to spare *me*, who knows you so well, the usual moonshine."

"Felix . . ." the earl began again.

"The pity is Sophia does not know you as well as I. She has not heard you boast of filling chits with flummery until they act the mooncalf. She has not heard you laugh about their foolishness, as I have on so many occasions."

"Felix . . ." Sophia said gently, unable to understand his anger when it was patently obvious he was heels over head in love with Manuela Malliende.

The young man cast her a withering look. "I had thought you different to the green girls and foolish matrons who fling themselves at my cousin's head."

"I love him, Felix!" she blurted out, and the young man's lips twisted into a travesty of a smile.

"Then you are indeed to be pitied." Addressing himself once again to his cousin he went on, "You just had to win the wager, even though I declined to take it up, didn't you?" The earl looked shocked as Felix added, "Well, I own you have won and you will have the thousand guineas on the morrow."

Sophia got to her feet then, her brow furrowed with perplexity. "Wager? What wager? What are you on about?"

Felix turned to her then, smiling triumphantly. "Naturally you would not know of it."

"Tell me," she snapped.

"When my heroic coz returned to town and learned of our betrothal, he wagered me one thousand guineas that you would not remain faithful to me until the end of the Season. Naturally I took exception to it and he apparently withdrew, but it is now very evident he was determined to be proved correct. My felicitations, Manville."

"Felix, this is a nonsense," the earl declared, but the young man had already turned on his heel and was striding back toward the rest of the guests.

Sophia looked at the earl then, her eyes filled

with hurt and bewilderment. "Is it true about the wager?"

"Sophia, I assure you . . ."

"Oh, save your lies for those foolish enough to believe them," she cried, wringing her hands in anguish. "You worked against us from the beginning. I should not be at all surprised if you encouraged Felix to fall in love with your protégée."

"If I did it was only because I coveted you for myself," he answered softly.

But Sophia did not hear his last words as she rushed from his side, brushing past Felix, feeling that if she did not escape this place her heart would break into a thousand pieces. For a very short time she had experienced ecstasy, but now she couldn't ever imagine being happy again.

Fifteen

"I cannot conceive what possessed you to do such a crack-brained thing," Lady Kingsland declared as she stared in dismay at her elder daughter over the breakfast table.

Sophia sat with a piece of untouched bread and butter on her plate and a full cup of coffee at her elbow. She had never felt less like eating.

"Felix and I have decided it would be foolish to proceed with our plans to marry, after all, Mama, and I had little choice but to write to him and terminate our betrothal. It is not so unusual for couples to change their minds, you must own."

"For others it may not be unusual, but you and Felix Harcourt are perfectly matched," her mother complained. "None more so."

"Felix, I believe is too young for matrimony and I accepted his offer far too soon after my come out."

"What will happen to *my* come out if Sophia is

not wed by the end of the Season?" Jessica moaned. "I could not bear it to be delayed another year."

"You need have no fear," her sister assured her. "I can always join the Convent of St. Agatha and your come out need not be delayed at all."

"A convent!" her mother and sister chorused in unison.

Sophia looked down at her plate. "It would be the ideal solution, for I have no wish to associate with gentlemen ever again."

"What a chucklehead you are," her sister reproved, "and all because Felix fancies himself in love with an opera-dancer. He will have forgotten her within the sennight."

"I have never known such foolishness," Lady Kingsland agreed. "Why, I recall when your papa . . . Well, that is of no account now. I am bound to agree with Jessica on this point. You have, my dear girl, acted with undue haste and will live to regret it."

"If Felix falls out of love with Senorita Malliende today, it will not alter my feelings about our marriage," Sophia declared. "It is over between us and nothing can change that."

"You could at least receive Lord Manville when he calls," Jessica told her.

As Sophia stiffened at the mention of his name, Lady Kingsland added, "No doubt he only wishes to plead his cousin's case, but you could receive him, Sophia. There is no cause to cut *him*."

Sophia continued to look down at her plate. "There really is no point as I am not like to change my mind, and I do suspect Lord Manville's part in this business."

Her mother sighed deeply. "Well, I own he has been guilty of far worse. However, you should have a thought for your future and I doubt if life as a nun will suit. You have cried off every diversion since the Prince's ball, and I tell you, Sophia, it will not do. The tattle-baskets will be making much out of this."

"Let them," Sophia declared, looking defiant, "and pray ask Papa to put a notice in the *Gazette* to make it absolutely plain Felix and I are no longer engaged to be married."

"I vouchsafe you will live to regret this piece of recklessness," her mother warned once again. "It is not as if you encouraged others to be hopeful. Felix Harcourt was your first and last suitor."

"Let that be a lesson to you, Jess," her sister warned.

"Oh, you may be certain I intend to be a shameless flirt and take my time to choose. Therein lies the fun, but you are not of the same mind, I feel. Given the chance, you would do exactly the same again."

"Being a spinster in our society is a sorry state of affairs," Lady Kingsland lamented.

"It cannot possibly be worse than being leg-shackled to a treacherous male," Sophia responded in heartfelt tones.

Lady Kingsland once again drew a deep sigh. "I can see you will not listen to reason on this matter. Perchance it is too soon after the event."

"I would appreciate a respite, Mama. Nothing can be resolved by discussion now. What is done cannot be undone and no one is more regretful than I am."

"At least you will have more time to devote to

mundane matters." Sophia experienced a small measure of relief. "Mayhap you will be good enough to go to Mr. Franklin's emporium to buy some braiding for my new pelisse this morning."

The suggestion left Sophia looking dismayed. "Mama, I hoped to stay at home and read my new novel."

"I will not allow you to gainsay me in this, Sophia. You might feel it necessary to cry off social diversions, but you have not stepped outside this house since the ball and you are beginning to look exceedingly pale."

"The weather has not been clement, Mama."

"Nevertheless it has now improved and I wish you to go."

Recognizing the resolve in her mother's voice, Sophia drew a deep sigh. "Have you no thought for my sensibilities, Mama?"

"Your sensibilities will not in the least be affected by your doing an errand for me."

"They will if I encounter acquaintances like Celia Waddell."

"Did you know that Senorita Malliende may never dance again?" Jessica asked in an effort to divert the conversation to a safer topic.

Sophia looked all at once shocked, for she had been so steeped in her own misery she had scarce given a thought to Manuela Malliende since that dreadful evening at Carlton House.

"I am truly sorry to hear you say so," she responded. "Was she so badly injured? In truth I did not think so at the time."

"No one can say for certain," Jessica admitted, "but I have heard she is still resting at home and no date can be given for her next performance, which sounds exceedingly ominous to me."

"That is a dreadful shame," Lady Kingsland lamented.

"All in all, it was not a successful evening for any of us," Sophia remarked.

"You are very generous to say so," Jessica told her. "If I were you, I would wish Senorita Malliende all manner of ills."

"She cannot be blamed for what happened," Sophia explained. "Nor can Felix for that matter. We are both victims of our own passions."

"Indeed?" Jessica responded, looking intrigued. "And for whom do you feel passion, may I ask?"

"You mistake my meaning," Sophia replied crisply as she pushed back her chair and got up from the table.

However, she was aware that her sister's gaze followed her with interest until she had left the room.

Sophia completed her mother's shopping as swiftly as she could, despite being accosted by several acquaintances, the one thing she had dreaded. Fortunately it was not yet known that she and Felix had parted, so that Manuela Malliende's injury was the main topic of everyone's conversation.

Several people stopped Sophia to inquire of the dancer's condition, hoping she would have the latest news. She was only able to repeat, however, what Jessica had told her, which was what was already generally known. When she had, at last, completed her mother's errand, she sat in the carriage for several minutes before she found herself instructing the coachman to drive her to Tavistock Square.

As she climbed down from the carriage outside the house, she questioned her own sanity in calling upon the woman who was so prominent in both Lord Manville's life and that of Felix, but her concern all at once transcended her prejudice. In any event, it was not Manuela Malliende's fault that gentlemen found her bewitching.

When she was ushered into the flower-bedecked parlor, Sophia found her seated with her injured ankle resting on a silken cushion. With the air of an invalid she looked particularly appealing, but Sophia could only pity her just then.

Lady Truscott was doing her embroidery and both ladies greeted her warmly as Sophia hesitantly entered the room.

"It is providential that you chose today to call," Lady Truscott told her, "for the past three have been so hectic with all manner of callers. We should not have been able to have a coze."

"I am most concerned for the state of Senorita Malliende's health," Sophia told them truthfully, glancing at the girl. "How is your ankle?"

"Somewhat improved, I am glad to say. However, it is not yet known if it will be as good as it was, which is quite a concern to one of my calling, as you might imagine."

"What a dreadful thing to happen at the very moment of your greatest triumph," Sophia sympathized.

"It was mortifying, you may be sure," the dancer agreed.

"His Royal Highness's own physician has called

in every day," Lady Truscott informed her, "and he has specific orders to report back to the Prince on every occasion."

"It is generally held that the Prince has a kind heart," Sophia replied.

"He has been exceedingly kind to me," the dancer affirmed. "Indeed, everyone has been most concerned. I am overwhelmed, I confess."

"It is only your due," Sophia found herself saying.

"Among the many others, Mr. Harcourt has called in at regular intervals, but no doubt you already know that full well, Miss Kingsland."

It was evident that neither Lady Truscott nor Senorita Malliende knew she and Felix were no longer betrothed. For an instant Sophia welcomed the respite, but then acknowledged their estrangement would soon be public knowledge once the notice was placed in the *Gazette*. As Lady Truscott was Felix's aunt, and he had evidently not spoken to her of it, Sophia considered she must tell her before the news was made public.

Sophia toyed with her kid gloves. "He did not tell me, senorita. I have not seen Felix since the night of the Carlton House ball."

Lady Truscott looked at her curiously. "That does not sound in the least like Felix."

"I am sorry to have to tell you, ma'am, that our betrothal is now at an end."

As she made the announcement, Sophia watched Senorita Malliende carefully. Her eyes opened with surprise and it was difficult to discern whether she was sorry or glad, but she was certainly surprised.

Lady Truscott, however, gasped loudly and set down her sewing.

"I cannot credit this, Miss Kingsland. What can have gone amiss between you?"

"Nothing remarkable, ma'am. We simply acknowledged that after all we did not suit."

"I confess to being shocked, Miss Kingsland."

"I regret that above all else, ma'am."

"Tush! My feelings in this matter are of no account. You must not be so firmly persuaded that it is over."

"But I am, ma'am."

"Surely you may yet resolve your differences."

"I truly think not, ma'am."

"If Felix has been acting the rapscallion, he is in for a severe trimming from me."

Sophia smiled sadly. "You must not for anything think so, ma'am. If any blame is to be apportioned, it is to me. I cried off, not Felix."

"I am also truly shocked by this news," Senorita Malliende said at last. "Mr. Harcourt, whenever I was in his company, always spoke of you with such kind feeling."

"I trust he will continue to do so in the future," Sophia responded, "but we did not suit and it is as well we acknowledge the truth of that fact before our wedding."

"Many young couples part brass rags," Lady Truscott pointed out hopefully, "and regret doing so within a sennight."

"I fear that will not happen to us, ma'am," Sophia replied, "and I truly regret any pain our parting may have caused *you*." Then, getting to her feet, she said, "Pray excuse me; I have stayed longer than I intended."

"It has been a pleasure to see you, Miss Kingsland," Manuela Malliende told her, "except for your sad news, of course."

"As long as you are on your way to full recovery all will be well, senorita."

"Do call in again whenever you are able," the girl begged.

To her own surprise, Sophia found herself saying, "Indeed, I will, ma'am."

As she left the room, she caught sight of Lady Truscott shaking her head sadly. It was as well, Sophia reflected, she did not know of her other nephew's part in the matter. Whenever she recalled his behavior, an invisible dart jabbed at her heart, but she was determined none should ever know of her real heartache.

The house steward was just about to show her out when Felix came into the hall, sweeping off his high-crowned beaver. The moment he saw Sophia, however, his bright, expectant expression turned to one of apprehension.

"Sophia, this is a surprise."

"It does not in the least surprise me to see you here."

"Why have you come?" he asked, with some heightening of his color.

"Undoubtedly for the same reason as you. I came to inquire of Senorita Malliende's health."

"Oh . . . indeed. How good of you. Sophia," he went on quickly, looking troubled, "about the other evening . . ."

"It is no longer of any consequence," she assured him.

"I cannot tell you how I regret that matters have come to this sorry state. I cannot even begin to conceive how it happened."

"Well, it is quite obvious to me, I assure you!"

He looked so distraught then she actually found herself feeling sorry for him. "We were so happy, I recall, such a short time ago."

"We thought we were, but in truth it was not the happiness of those in love with each other," she told him gently. "You came to prefer another and so did I. No one can regret that more than I, Felix, but I am bound to say your choice was the wiser one, and I can only wish you happy."

"You are incredibly generous, Sophia. I don't deserve it. I should have challenged that scoundrel when I saw him using you so ill."

"What good would bloodshed do for any of us?" she asked sadly. "In any event I became aware of your attachment to Senorita Malliende before your cousin and I . . ."

Her voice tailed away and he put one hand out to her in a sympathetic gesture. "Oh, my dear . . ."

"Good luck, Felix," she murmured as she brushed past him, rushing out into the street and climbing into her carriage before she burst into another fit of weeping.

Before she even had an opportunity to sit down, she gasped with shock, for instead of Lily waiting for her in the carriage, she discovered the earl was seated in the corner, looking as cool and as relaxed as usual.

The shock caused Sophia to sink back rather

heavily into the squabs. Without saying a word, the earl indicated with a brief tap of his cane that the driver should set off, thus ensuring she could not get out once she had recovered from her surprise.

"What are *you* doing here?" she demanded, her voice still breathless.

"I wished to see you and as it became evident to me you would not allow me to call on you in the normal manner, desperate measures were called for."

"And where, may I ask, is my maidservant?"

His lips quirked into a smile at last. "I promise you I have not done anything wicked with her, my dear, despite my fearsome reputation."

Some of her outrage faded then. It was impossible for her to remain angry with him whatever he had done to hurt her.

"Now you are roasting me," she accused.

One dark eyebrow quirked upward. "You do not doubt my terrible reputation, do you?"

"You have given me no reason to do so."

"Well, at least you need harbor no fear for your abigail. The creature is safely on her way to your house in my curricle, so you may rest assured on her behalf."

Sophia turned away from him in exasperation. "Oh, I wonder you dare show your face."

"It is the only way I can impress upon you the truth of the matter, my dearest, dearest Sophia."

His use of her name in so gentle a tone smote at her heart. "I believe I already know the truth and I am wounded by it."

"I think you do not."

"You wagered Felix that I would not remain faithful to him until the end of the Season, and in a manner true to your nature, you ensured you won."

"I cannot deny that the wager was made, Sophia, or at least an attempt at one, but Felix did not accept and that was before I had met you formally. I beg of you to believe me when I tell you I forgot all about the cursed wager the moment Felix left my house."

She turned to face him again and he said softly, taking her hands in his, "My dearest Sophia, the reason I kissed you the other evening was because I had longed to do so since the moment we met, before I knew you were to marry my cousin. After I left you that day in Leeke Lane, I could not get you out of my mind, and I feared we should never meet again. Imagine my utter dismay when I discovered you were about to marry my cousin."

"If only I could believe you," she breathed.

His hands gripped hers more tightly so she could not withdraw them. "Look at me and you will surely know that I love you with all my heart."

She gazed longingly into his dark eyes and could see nothing but his own anxiety. There was nothing of the usual mockery and amusement in his manner. Even so she turned away, tearing her hands from his grasp at last.

"Oh, if only I could believe you did not tell every gullible female that tale."

"I have never told any female that I loved her," he vowed and she could discern nothing but sincerity in his manner.

Sophia ached to throw herself into his arms, but a mixture of pride and fear held her back.

"Trust me to make you happy, Sophia, and I vow

you will never know a day's regret in the future," he added.

When she still didn't respond, he drew her toward him, saying, "Devil take it! I am not going to accept a negative answer! You will marry me and well before the end of the Season. I am not prepared to wait!"

Once she was clasped in his arms, she could resist him no longer and they were still locked in a passionate embrace when the carriage drew into Manchester Square. It was not until the carriage came to a standstill that Sophia broke away from him.

"What of Senorita Malliende?" she asked breathlessly.

He looked a little surprised at her question. "I daresay in time she will come to appreciate my cousin's devotion, if she does not already do so."

"I am more concerned for *your* relationship with her," Sophia pointed out.

"The relationship, as you put it, my dearest love, is not what everyone would want to believe of us."

"If it was, you would not have tolerated Felix's behavior toward her. I have it in mind you would have been a trifle more proprietorial of her affections, but you must understand that I do want to know if there is more to the matter than her dancing."

"Quite simply, there is," he answered, his smile fading somewhat. "It was Manuela and her family who cared for me when I was so dreadfully injured. I owe her my life, Sophia. Manuela and her family nursed me devotedly."

"Oh, I had no notion."

"She would not wish me to speak of it. Such behavior is natural to them and not worthy of consideration."

"I understand now," she said softly.

"In Spain there was little hope for her to succeed as a dancer, or even to enjoy a normal life as yet, so it was agreed I would take her to London where I felt success was more or less assured for one so talented. However," he added, looking wry, "it was a surprise to both of us the extent of her success."

"Will she be able to dance again?"

"With Felix as her devoted love, I doubt if she will care so much, but the injury is thought to be slight. I believe she will make as complete a recovery as I did."

"For what she did for you in Spain, I shall be forever in her debt. Moreover, I am now consumed with guilt." He looked at her with surprise as she went on, "She has few true friends here in England and she intimated to me on more than the one occasion that she wished for us to become close. I, however, resisted her entreaties because I believe I was jealous of her."

"Because of her relationship to me or to Felix?"

"My foolish prejudice began well before Felix's infatuation, if I recall correctly."

He raised her hand to his lips as the lackey came to open the carriage door, "You will have ample opportunity to correct your misjudgment in the future."

"You may be sure that I will. Indeed, I shall look forward to it, but I am beginning to be in something of a quake at the thought of our news becoming known. All my acquaintances will consider me a slyboots."

The earl laughed as he gave her his hand. "The news is almost certain to cause a sensation, I am bound to agree."

"You are looking forward to it," she accused.

"I confess that I am. Do you mind?"

She gazed at him lovingly. "I care only that we love each other and very soon the entire world will know of it."

"Come then, I will speak with Sir Magnus and afterward we can inform Lady Kingsland that a wedding is to take place after all, and sooner than she believed."

Sophia felt incredibly lighthearted as he handed her down from the carriage. "Imagine their surprise! No one will be more delighted than Mama, and Jessica, who will now face no delay in her come out."

"No one could be happier than we two, Sophia," he corrected as they approached the front door.

"We must be the happiest couple in the entire world!" she declared as they went inside to impart the good news to the Kingsland family.

PASSION
&
ROMANCE
FROM
RACHELLE
EDWARDS